D1507238

A Spring to Remember

Don't miss the place where
the adventures began!

ICE CREAM SUMMER

ONCE UPON A WINTER

A FALL FOR FRIENDSHIP

· AN ORCHARD NOVEL ·

A SPRING TO REMEMBER

By Megan Atwood

Illustrated by Natalie Andrewson

ALADDIN

New York London Toronto Sydney New Delhi

This book is a work of fiction. Any references to historical events, real people, or real places are used fictitiously. Other names, characters, places, and events are products of the author's imagination, and any resemblance to actual events or places or persons, living or dead, is entirely coincidental.

ALADDIN

An imprint of Simon & Schuster Children's Publishing Division

1230 Avenue of the Americas, New York, New York 10020

First Aladdin hardcover edition January 2019

Text copyright © 2019 by Simon & Schuster, Inc.

Illustrations copyright © 2019 by Natalie Andrewson

All rights reserved, including the right of reproduction in whole or in part in any form.

ALADDIN and related logo are registered trademarks of Simon & Schuster, Inc.

For information about special discounts for bulk purchases, please contact Simon & Schuster Special Sales at 1-866-506-1949 or business@simonandschuster.com.

The Simon & Schuster Speakers Bureau can bring authors to your live event. For more information or to book an event contact the Simon & Schuster Speakers Bureau at 1-866-248-3049 or visit our website at www.simonspeakers.com.

Book designed by Laura Lyn DiSiena

The illustrations for this book were rendered digitally.

The text of this book was set in Baskerville.

Manufactured in the United States of America 1218 FFG

10 9 8 7 6 5 4 3 2 1

Library of Congress Cataloging-in-Publication Data

Names: Atwood, Megan, author. | Andrewson, Natalie, illustrator.

Title: A spring to remember / by Megan Atwood ; illustrated by Natalie Andrewson.

Description: First Aladdin hardcover/paperback edition. | New York : Aladdin, 2019. | Series: An Orchard novel ; 4 | Summary: Lizzie reluctantly goes along with a series of matchmaking schemes, even though she is not sure the couples actually want their help. | Identifiers: LCCN 2018039979 (print) | LCCN 2018046505 (eBook) | ISBN 9781481490542 (eBook) | ISBN 9781481490535 (hardcover)

Subjects: | CYAC: Friendship—Fiction. | Assertiveness (Psychology)—Fiction. | Dating services—Fiction. | BISAC: JUVENILE FICTION / Social Issues / Friendship. | JUVENILE FICTION / Nature & the Natural World / Environment. | JUVENILE FICTION / Humorous Stories.

Classification: LCC PZ7.A8952 (eBook) | LCC PZ7.A8952 Sp 2019 (print) | DDC [Fic]—dc23

LC record available at https://lccn.loc.gov/2018039979

To Mom and Dad, always

A SPRING to REMEMBER

CHAPTER 1

Right in the Kisser

Lizzie sneezed, sending glitter swirling through the air to land all over her family's big dining room table. When she opened her eyes, the whole Valentine's Day Orchard Dance Decoration and Party Crew—or so they'd taken to calling themselves—were staring at her. Granted, it was just her parents and her three best friends in the world looking at her. But having everyone's attention was not Lizzie's thing. Her face got hot.

1

"Sorry," she said quietly, and rubbed her nose.

Her dad grinned. "I think even your sneezes are sounding more musical!" He nudged his wife, and Lizzie's mother smiled big.

Lizzie pretended she didn't hear them. They were talking about the singing lessons they'd made her sign up for—to find her "voice," they said. Lizzie thought the lessons were a terrible idea and felt just fine keeping quiet.

"The Valentine's Day Orchard Dance Decoration and Party Crew forgives you!" Sarah, one of her three best friends, said.

Her other best friend Olive said, "You have glitter on your nose, Lizzie," and pushed her glasses up, getting glitter on her own nose.

Before Lizzie could say anything, Peter—her other *other* best friend—snorted at Olive, and the two of them shared some look that Lizzie couldn't understand. They were twins and they were always doing that. But Sarah finished Lizzie's sentences all the time, so she knew the feeling, at least.

Peter asked Lizzie's parents, "So, in the fall the Garrison Orchard does a whole fall thing with a pumpkin patch and haunted house—"

"And zombie hayrides!" Sarah yelled.

Peter shot her a look, and Sarah looked down sheepishly. Peter and Olive had moved fairly recently to New Amity, and Lizzie and Sarah had immediately wanted to be friends with them. Well, Lizzie had. Sarah was a whole different story, but she'd come around. Peter had started off super-shy—almost as shy as Lizzie—but after a bit of a harrowing ordeal, he'd really come out of his shell. And part of that was pushing back at

Sarah's always interrupting. Sarah could be . . . well, Lizzie would call it "enthusiastic."

Peter went on, "And in the winter, you have the sleigh rides and the whole holiday display and the party and you sell things in the shop. . . ."

Olive said, "Don't forget the ice cream stand and all the tours and stuff in the summer." She didn't even look up when she said it. She was drawing a heart with glue and concentrating hard.

Peter sighed. "I'm getting there, Olive!" Lizzie smiled, and now it was her and Peter's turn to share a look. As the two quieter ones in the group, they often got talked over. Or "reminded" of things.

"And the ice cream stand and all that in the summer. But in the spring, it's just the Valentine's Day Dance? Is there anything else we'll be doing?" Peter asked.

Lizzie loved that he'd said "we." Nothing made her happier than sharing the orchard—her home—with the friends she loved. She knew the answer, but she let her parents do the talking.

"You're asking why we're only doing a dance on Valentine's Day and nothing else until summer, when every other season is a huge production? Good question," Lizzie's mom said. "And the answer is . . . by this time in the year, we're pretty tired." She laughed, and Albert snorted. "And we need just a little break. So we make one BIG event in the spring, or sort of spring. This is kind of our last hurrah until the summer stand and veggies, and the whole town comes to say goodbye until then, basically. Goodbye to the big productions, anyway."

"And then we sleep for days," Lizzie's dad finished, grinning.

5

"So we have to keep making more decorations. The dance will get here before we know it!" her mom said. "Get on it, people." She winked at the group. But Lizzie knew she really meant it.

Olive looked up and pushed up her glasses. "I'm out of glue. Does anyone have any more?"

Peter looked around and shrugged.

Sarah said, "I'm glue-less." Then she looked around, smiling. Lizzie cracked up, putting her hand over her mouth. Peter and Olive laughed and shook their heads. "Get it?" Sarah went on. "Instead of CLUE-less?"

Olive rolled her eyes but smiled. "Yeah, yeah, we got it. No more glue anywhere?"

Lizzie looked around and saw all the glue sticks in the throw-out pile. She looked at her parents. "Should we get more?"

Her mom nodded. "Yeah, would you mind? You four run into town and grab some more. But you have to hurry, Lizzie. You don't want to be late for your singing lesson!"

Lizzie looked down and didn't say anything. She *absolutely* wanted to be late for her singing lesson. Maybe she'd be so late, it would even be canceled.

"ON IT," Sarah yelled. "We'll be fast!" The four of them ran to get their coats. In February, New Hampshire was still in the dead of winter. But Lizzie loved how even in the frigid air, you could feel spring just starting to come.

They burst through the door of the Garrisons' great big house and sprinted down the driveway, Lizzie a few steps behind. When they got to the end of the long driveway, they slowed down and walked past the wooden fences of the orchard toward the main street. Lizzie caught up with her friends just as Sarah was saying something.

"—really weird and I think we need to figure out what's happening."

Lizzie said, a little out of breath, "What's weird?"

"My mom," Sarah said. "She's been acting weird. Weirder than usual, anyway."

Lizzie had to admit Sarah's mom, Ms. Shirvani, was pretty . . . pretty out there. As the town librarian, Sarah's mom was probably the smartest person Lizzie had ever met. But sometimes she was a little spacey. But then again, Lizzie had an older sister—Gloria—who yelled the word "ACTING" all the time and walked around in different costumes, so who was she to judge?

"Weird how?" Olive asked, pushing up her glasses.

"Oh, she's just spending all her time with

Sheriff Hadley and she's really giggly all the time. And even spacier."

Lizzie felt her eyes go wide, and she tried not to look at Olive and Peter. It seemed that Sarah was the only person who didn't know that Sarah's mom and Sheriff Hadley were dating. Lizzie didn't know why Ms. Shirvani didn't just tell her daughter. Sarah loved Sheriff Hadley already.

They had reached Main Street, and Sarah turned to face the three of them. "Anyway, I think we should do some . . . what's that word? Isn't there a word for spying? I think my mom used it once. Recognize? Regongan?"

Olive said, "Reconnaissance," and Lizzie turned to her in surprise.

"*What* is that word?" Lizzie asked. "Recond-a-nance?"

"Re-CON-a-sance," Olive said, sounding it out. She shrugged. "I like reading the dictionary sometimes."

Peter nodded. "Sometimes our family does that for fun."

Lizzie smiled. That sounded exactly like something their family would do. They were always experimenting and looking things up. Lizzie loved that they did that but was super-glad her own family just watched movies for fun.

Sarah continued, "Anyway, I think we should spy on her a little bit. Something is up."

Just as she spoke, behind her and three shops down, Sheriff Hadley and Sarah's mother stepped out of Dinah's Diner. Lizzie felt an elbow in her side, and she nodded without looking—Olive had spotted them too.

They'd stopped in the middle of the sidewalk. Ms. Shirvani moved in closer to the sheriff and then . . . they were kissing.

Lizzie's face flushed as she thought about what this might mean to Sarah. She felt a squeak jump out of her, and she clapped her hand over her mouth.

"What the heck?" Sarah said. "Why do you all look like you've seen the ghost of Verity Wentworth?" She followed Lizzie's gaze and turned around.

Everything went quiet for a moment, and then Sarah said, much more softly than Lizzie had ever heard her speak, "Well. I guess we don't need to spy anymore." And she turned back around to them, her face pale and her eyes huge.

CHAPTER 2
Room 128

Lizzie squeaked again—she couldn't help it. Sometimes, even though she was quiet, the sounds just came out.

Sarah said, "Whgluroisd," her eyes still wide.

Olive and Peter both looked confused, but Lizzie knew what Sarah meant. Lizzie said quietly, "She said, 'What is happening?'" Sarah nodded.

Lizzie took a deep breath. Her best friend

needed her—she had to step up and get her through this shock, and through any of the anger she'd feel in a minute. Lizzie was in familiar territory: Take care of Sarah. Calm her down. Be a good friend.

"Let's get her back to the house. We can get glue later." Lizzie put her arm around Sarah and turned her so she wouldn't have Sheriff Hadley and Ms. Shirvani in her eyesight anymore—they were still kissing. Sarah made a little noise, but Lizzie patted her shoulder.

"It's okay," she said. "We're going to get you through this." She began to walk Sarah back toward the Garrisons' house. She made eye contact with Olive and Peter, who followed without saying a word.

Lizzie was about to start consoling Sarah when she heard the sound of a car coming. Looking up, she saw that it was her parents' car. For a minute, she was completely confused. But then her heart sank. She knew what would come next.

The car reached them and Lizzie tightened her grip on Sarah's shoulder. Her mom rolled down the car window and said, "It's time for your first singing lesson, Lizzie! Hop in."

Lizzie swallowed. "Mom, I need to take—"

"Nope," her mom said. "You need to get in right now."

"Mom, Sarah just—"

"Sarah will be fine," her mom said firmly. She looked at Sarah. "Won't you, Sarah?"

Sarah said, "Bhriswet."

Her mom said, "See? Get in."

Lizzie geared up to argue more, but her mom said in her "don't argue" voice, "NOW, Lizzie."

Lizzie huffed and shot Sarah a look that said, "I'M SO SORRY!" and Sarah said, "Brlg." Lizzie got into the car and put on her seat belt, then watched helplessly as Olive and Peter took over and guided Sarah down the road.

Lizzie crossed her arms over her chest and refused to look at her mom. She concentrated on the New Amity Main Street going by—the sheriff and Ms. Shirvani were no longer on the sidewalk. The thought made a fresh wave of irritation slide through her. She could be helping Sarah right now, but instead she was stuck going to something she didn't even want to go to.

After a few minutes of driving, her mom said, "Sarah will be fine, I'm sure, but she did look a little upset. Is everything okay?"

Lizzie closed her eyes and sighed. She opened her mouth to speak, but her mother interrupted.

"These lessons are going to be so great for you, honey. Your father and I are always talking about how you need to find your voice. And then we came up with the idea for these singing lessons and it was like a light-bulb went on!"

Lizzie sighed and stopped trying to talk. It

wasn't any use. Her mom would just talk right over her. And it looked like the singing lesson was going to happen no matter what, because the passing landscape had gone from farmland to more and more houses and then finally to the downtown of Monroeville—New Amity's bigger sister town.

Her mom found parking near an old-looking building that had the name MONROE-VILLE MUSIC CENTER. Lizzie's stomach flipped and her mouth went dry. She tried to say something to her mom, but her mom had already gotten out of the car and stood waiting by the driver's-side door, taking in the building. Lizzie closed her eyes and drew in a deep breath. She got out of the car and walked to her mom like a puppy walking to its kennel.

"Look at how beautiful this building is, Lizzie!" her mom said, walking briskly to the entrance. Lizzie had to half run to catch up. "And you can hear the music in here and everything."

Sure enough, when they opened the front doors, a wave of warm air met them along with all different types of musical sounds. Lizzie heard someone singing "La la la la la la," going from low to high notes. She also heard a violin hitting some wrong notes and heard drums pounding somewhere. Her mom looked thrilled, and she rubbed Lizzie's back excitedly.

"So much movement and music happening

here, Lizzie. Won't this be fun? I should bring Gloria here too. . . ."

Lizzie stopped listening to her mom and thought about Sarah. She had no doubt this would NOT be fun. And all she wanted to do was go help her friend. A fresh wave of resentment rose through her. But she had no time to say anything because her mom had moved to the front desk in the lobby and was talking to the receptionist. He waved toward the long hallway and the tons of shut doors that lined its walls and said, "Room 128." Lizzie's mom beckoned to her, then started down the hall. Lizzie caught up again just in time for her mom to open the door to room 128 and stride in.

Lizzie stood where she was for a moment. She felt like crying. But she had a feeling that the longer she stood in the hall, the longer the lesson would last. And she had to go back to help Sarah. She squared her shoulders and walked into room 128.

CHAPTER 3
Spit It Out!

T his must be the wonderful Lizzie!" said an older man with a white mustache and kind, crinkly eyes when Lizzie walked in.

Lizzie swallowed and stood just a little bit behind her mom. Her mom beamed and said, "Yep, this is my baby! One of them, anyway. She's so excited to start these lessons."

Lizzie looked down and then tried to muster a smile. When she looked up, the man was looking at her with those kind crinkly eyes, and he had a small knowing smile on his face. "Okay, then, let's get going, shall we? I'm Mr. Samson," he said, and put his hand out to shake. He bowed a little when he did and gave her a goofy smile, and when she shook his hand he pumped it up and down really big. Lizzie giggled a little and her shoulders relaxed. She realized they'd been practically up to her ears.

Her mom kissed her on the head and said, "All right, I'll skedaddle. Be back in an hour, Lizziebean. Can't wait to hear how it goes!" She winked at Lizzie and left the room and it was just Lizzie and Mr. Samson.

Lizzie took a minute to look around the room. The building was old and the walls were white brick. There was a whole wall of windows that looked over a courtyard with bushes and trees partially covered in snow. In the middle of the room was a small upright black piano, which Mr. Samson sat down at, playing a couple of notes. Various instruments and chairs lined the walls, but Mr. Samson pointed to a chair that sat next to the piano. Lizzie cleared her throat, walked over, and sat down, her stomach going crazy and her face already flushing.

"So!" Mr. Samson said, turning on the bench toward her. He clasped his hands and smiled at her. "What made you decide to take singing lessons?"

Lizzie opened her mouth and then closed it. She wasn't prepared for this question somehow. She supposed some people liked to sing. . . . People like her sister, Gloria, would probably love

25

something like this. Singing lessons had just never occurred to her until her parents said she had to take them. She wasn't quite sure what to say.

"Uh," she said.

"Yes," said Mr. Samson. "Your parents signed you up, right?" Lizzie nodded and he sighed. "You're not the first student I've had who is here because their parents thought it was a good idea."

Lizzie smiled and looked down. That made her feel a little better.

Mr. Samson went on, "The question is, did your parents think you should come here because they've heard you singing and thought you had some skill to develop, or was it for some other reason? Let's just do some really easy, quick scales to see where you are, shall we?"

Lizzie's stomach flopped again and she felt

really hot all of a sudden. The truth was—and she had never even told Sarah this—she actually really liked to sing. But she was sure she didn't have any special talent or anything. And she NEVER wanted to sing in front of anyone. This was pretty much her nightmare. Well, almost. If there were people staring at her and everyone expected her to sing perfectly at some event—THAT would be her nightmare. She hoped with all her heart that nothing like that would ever happen.

"I'm going to hit a note on this piano and then sing a note, and I want to see if you can match it, okay?" Mr. Samson said.

Lizzie couldn't say anything, so she just nodded.

He hit the first note and sang, "Laaaa," looking at Lizzie expectantly.

She opened her mouth and sang . . . nothing.

It was like her voice had disappeared. He nodded and smiled at her. "It's okay. Try again." He pressed the piano key and sang, "Laaaa."

Lizzie sang, *crooooaaakkk*. She felt her eyes go wide and she slapped a hand over her mouth. Why wouldn't her voice work?

"I'm sorry!" she said, and then was surprised that she could say THAT but not sing one note.

Mr. Samson chuckled and said, "It's okay, Lizzie. This happens. It's scary to sing in front of someone for the first time. We'll keep trying." He hit the note on the piano. "Laaaaaa."

Lizzie opened her mouth and sang, *squeeeaaak*. She slapped a hand over her mouth again, and she could actually feel how hot her face was and could imagine how beet red she must be.

This was going much worse than she'd thought

it could. Which was saying something, since she had been expecting pretty much the worst. And somehow, this was way worse than even that.

Mr. Samson frowned, but not in a mean way, and said, "Okay, I think we should try something else." He swiveled all the way around to face her.

Lizzie felt like crying. Was it possible she was failing to sing even one note? How could she have failed this badly so soon?

But Mr. Samson's kind eyes and nice smile made her relax a little. He didn't seem mad—not at all.

"Can I just ask you some questions, Ms. Lizzie?" he said.

She nodded. Though she hoped she could actually form words and answers to his questions.

"What's your favorite holiday?" he asked.

Lizzie blinked. She was expecting questions like "What songs do you sing?" or "How come you're so bad at singing one note?"

The question surprised her so much, she didn't even think about how mortified she was about the whole situation. "Halloween," she said immediately.

Mr. Samson's eyes widened. "Yes! Mine too! What do you like about it?"

Lizzie shifted in her seat and leaned forward. "Um, I like what we do at the orchard. And how spooky things are," she said. And then she thought that might be a really dumb answer.

But Mr. Samson nodded enthusiastically. "Right! My favorite thing to do is take walks around Halloween time to see everyone's decorations. And the weather is great," he said.

Lizzie said, "I know! I like wearing sweaters and drinking hot apple cider. And seeing the leaves, but also seeing how spooky it can get when the fog settles on our fields."

"That's right, you mentioned the orchard! I've been there, you know. It's one of my favorite places to be in the fall. I didn't get a chance to go this past autumn—did you do anything special?"

Lizzie nodded so big her head felt like it might fall off. "We did! My friends and I and my sister, Gloria, and her friends put on a play and a haunted house. And there was a zombie hayride. And we think there was a real ghost in our barn. And spooky things kept happening around the orchard, so we had to figure things out and had to help the ghost move on. Her name was Verity Wentworth, and she used to live at our farm a long, long time ago. And we dressed up and handed out candy. . . ." All of a sudden Lizzie realized that she was talking a lot and stopped. Most people didn't let her talk this long.

But Mr. Samson nodded and his eyes were wide. "A real ghost? That sounds both scary and thrilling!"

Lizzie said, "It was! But my friends and I were pretty brave. Well, at least my friends were." She ducked her head and felt her face get hot again.

Mr. Samson said, "It sounds like you were brave too, though."

Lizzie shrugged. She was starting to feel a little uncomfortable again.

"Who are your friends?" Mr. Samson asked. "Do you all get to spend a lot of time together?"

Lizzie nodded. "Oh, yes. Sarah is my best

friend since forever and she's at our house all the time. Peter and Olive are twins and they moved here a little while ago and became our best friends. We do everything together," she said. Then thoughts about Sarah crept in. She blurted out, "I'm worried about Sarah."

She sank into herself a little, embarrassed she'd said something so personal. But Mr. Samson nodded. "I bet you're a good friend, huh?"

Lizzie shrugged again, and a little smile tugged at the corner of her mouth.

"Aha. I think we figured out what you really like to do. Be a good friend?"

She nodded but couldn't seem to look up.

Mr. Samson's voice got quiet. "Sometimes, when we're really good friends, we forget that we have our own ideas about what we want to do. Or we forget to do nice things for ourselves, too."

Lizzie swallowed and thought about that for a minute.

"But we can talk about that later. Can you believe it? Time is up!" Lizzie glanced at the clock in the corner, and sure enough, a whole hour had already passed. She couldn't believe it.

"I . . . didn't . . . ," she started.

Mr. Samson finished, "Sing a note? Yeah, that happens a lot the first lesson. This is all a part of the process!" He stood up and bowed to Lizzie. "Thank you, Ms. Lizzie, for sharing your thoughts with me. That's a type of art right there, just like making music is." He walked toward the door and opened it. "If you feel like it, you can practice singing along to songs you like until next time. Sound good? See you next week?"

Lizzie nodded and walked past him. When she got halfway down the hall, Mr. Samson called out, "Don't forget to take care of yourself while you're being a good friend, okay?"

Lizzie turned around and smiled. "Okay, Mr. Samson."

He beamed. "Okay."

Smiling the whole way, Lizzie walked to where her mother was parked outside. The singing lesson hadn't been so bad after all.

She got into the car and her mom said, "Well? How'd it go? Did you have fun?"

For the first time in a while, Lizzie could tell the truth enthusiastically. "Yeah, I really did."

Her mom put the car in drive and said smugly, "See, I knew you would."

Lizzie just smiled.

CHAPTER 4
A Strange Proposal

The whole way home, Lizzie tried to prepare for the disaster that was waiting for her there. Sarah would be devastated, that much she knew. Lizzie had suspected for some time that Ms. Shirvani and Sheriff Hadley were dating. She was always surprised when she knew something someone else didn't, though that happened a lot, especially if it had to do with people. And especially if Sarah was involved. Sarah tended not to notice a whole lot around her.

It had been a whole hour—more, even. Enough time for Sarah to get really worked up and worried and angry. Lizzie would have to really step up for her, she just knew. So when her mom pulled into their driveway, Lizzie stepped out of the car like a soldier on a mission.

She walked into the house, ready to deal with any yelling or crying that might be happening.

Instead, she heard excited voices in the living room.

She heard SARAH's excited voice in the living room.

Lizzie stopped in her tracks for a minute. It was so much the opposite of what she expected, she wondered if she'd imagined the encounter with the sheriff and Ms. Shirvani. Or if she had walked into the wrong house. She looked around—yep, it was her house, all right. And her mother had walked in behind her and was hanging up her keys and talking on the phone to someone. Lizzie shook her head, as if to shake the weirdness away.

She walked to the banister, tapped it three times like everyone did when they walked into the house, and then went to the living room, toward the excited voices. What she found there almost blew her mind.

Peter, Olive, and Sarah had thrown all the pillows on the floor like they always did when they had slumber parties or when they were planning big things. Sarah was talking, her hands gesturing wildly and her eyes bright. She,

Olive, and Peter heard Lizzie come in, and they all turned their heads toward her at exactly the same time.

They had huge smiles on their faces.

"LIZZIE!" Sarah yelled. "FINALLY. We have so much to talk about."

Lizzie didn't know what to say. That was an understatement.

"How come—" she started.

"—I'm not upset?" Sarah finished.

Lizzie nodded and then dropped onto a cushion near Peter.

"Well, I couldn't talk for a little bit," Sarah said. "Which isn't like me, I know."

Peter, Olive, and Lizzie all nodded at her. Olive said, "SO true," and grinned, but Sarah went on like she hadn't heard her.

"And it was a huge shock. I mean, who would have guessed?"

Lizzie and Olive shared a look but didn't say anything. Lizzie saw Peter stifling a smile.

Sarah went on, "But then I REALLY thought about it. Like, really. And guess what? I think it's a GREAT idea. Who's better than Sheriff Hadley?"

Relief flooded Lizzie. She absolutely agreed— she'd just thought it would be a much longer journey to get Sarah to think that way.

"I have so much fun with Sheriff Hadley. And I've always wanted to go to one of his sci-fi conventions, all dressed up. We both love *Doctor Who* and *Star Wars*. And now he'll have to take me! He'll be my stepdad if he and my mom get married!" Sarah stopped like the idea had just occurred to her. She added, almost like an afterthought, "I've never had a dad."

Peter said, "You can always borrow one of ours. We have two." They all giggled at this.

Sarah laughed, but her expression hadn't changed. "Sheriff Hadley as my stepdad," she almost whispered.

Olive said, businesslike, "We've been trying to figure out how long they've been going out. We think it's a year. Like right when Peter and I got here."

Lizzie glanced at Sarah and shook her head. "I think it's longer," she said.

Sarah said, "Wait, you've known this for a while and you never said anything to me?"

Lizzie sighed and thought about what she

wanted to say. Finally, she said, "I wasn't sure. I just guessed. They were always looking at each other and laughing. And one time, about a year before Peter and Olive got here, I saw her lean into him a little bit. And he leaned into her back. But sometimes WE all lean into each other as friends, so I couldn't tell for sure. And I didn't want to say anything."

Sarah furrowed her eyebrows. "I wish you'd said something," she said.

Lizzie's stomach dropped. Had she been a bad friend? She'd thought she was doing Sarah a favor. But maybe she'd made the wrong decision.

Olive jumped in. "But if she'd been wrong, then you would have been upset. Since those things could just be what close friends do."

Lizzie shot Olive a grateful look, and Olive smiled back at her.

Sarah nodded. "That's true. You were being a good friend by not getting my hopes up, I guess." She didn't look totally sure, but Lizzie breathed a sigh of relief anyway.

Sarah's eyebrows furrowed again. "Why didn't THEY tell me?" she asked.

Peter shrugged. "I've been wondering that too."

"Yeah," Olive said. "Do you think they thought you might be upset or something?"

"Well . . . ," Sarah said. "Sometimes I can be a little dramatic. At least that's what my mom says." She cleared her throat.

Lizzie looked down and didn't meet Sarah's eyes. She did, however, see that both Peter and Olive had looked down too.

Olive said, "Maybe you should just tell them you saw them kissing and that you're happy about it."

Sarah shook her head slowly. She drew herself up and said, "I have a better idea." She paused and made sure everyone was looking at her. She took a deep breath and said, "I think they should get married!"

No one said anything for a second. Olive pushed her glasses up her nose. "Okay. So maybe you should tell them you saw them kissing and that you're happy about it and you think they should get married."

Lizzie nodded. She wasn't quite sure why Sarah had been so . . . well, dramatic about saying they should get married.

But Sarah shook her head. "Oh, no. They

can't know I know. Not if they didn't want me to know. What if that breaks the spell and then they split up?"

Lizzie and Peter exchanged confused looks. Olive said, "I'm not sure that logic makes—"

"It's the only way to make sure they get married!" Sarah said, gesturing wildly. "We have to make THEM want to get married. We need to do some superspy work and figure out how to do that. Are you in?" she asked.

Lizzie said, "Uh . . ."

Olive said, "I'm not sure *what* we're in."

And Peter said at the same time, "What are we talking about?"

Sarah said, "AWESOME! Sunday—that's tomorrow, remember—I'll give you your assignments. We WILL get them to propose—and soon!"

Lizzie wasn't so sure. And she wasn't sure why Sarah needed this to happen right that instant. Or why she wouldn't just talk to her mom. But like Mr. Samson had said, Lizzie was a good friend.

"Okay," she said, squaring her shoulders. "We're in."

CHAPTER 5

Glorialand

After her friends left, Lizzie climbed the stairs to her room and flopped on her bed. She felt . . . off. Nothing seemed right. Here she was, a player in one of Sarah's complicated schemes again. Sarah tended to do this—take a simple solution and make it really hard. The difference now was that Lizzie had Olive and Peter: she really wanted to know what they thought. Maybe all three of them together could talk Sarah down. She decided to call them right then, even though they had just left.

Before she could do anything, though, her door flung open and her sister stood in the door-frame. She had on a boa and her sunglasses and she leaned in.

"*Baby*. I hear you had a voice lesson today," she said.

Lizzie furrowed her eyebrows. "Okay . . . ?" she said, her voice going up in a question. "Also, Mom said you're supposed to ask people if you can come in, instead of barging in." If Lizzie had flung open Gloria's door, Gloria would have screamed bloody murder.

Gloria waved her hand dismissively. "I am a student of the human experience, *baby*. How can I see humans in their natural habitats unless I catch them unaware? You wouldn't understand."

Lizzie couldn't argue with that. It sounded like her sister was saying she was an alien . . . that would explain a lot, but still she couldn't help but say, "You know YOU'RE human, right?"

Gloria ignored her and sat in the rocking chair next to a window. She looked out of it forlornly, as if she were looking at a ship sailing away with her best friend on it.

She sighed and took off her sunglasses, turning toward Lizzie. "I just want to know, *baby*, how it is you talked our parents into giving you voice lessons. They, sadly, cannot see that those lessons, out of the two of us, would better serve *me*. Even though I've desperately wanted singing lessons for an entire week now!"

Lizzie frowned. "Isn't that when they told

you I was going to be taking the lessons?"

Again, Gloria waved her hand. "No matter. The *point* is: Why are you getting lessons when you so clearly do not have a voice of your own anyway and will certainly not use them? Whereas I, a supremely talented actress already at my young age, would use these lessons to become even more amazing?"

Lizzie rolled her eyes and flopped back on her bed. Of course her sister was mad that Lizzie got lessons—Gloria hated anything that didn't involve her. And admittedly these lessons were way more suited to Gloria than to Lizzie. But something Gloria said rankled Lizzie, and she sat up again. "I do too have a voice!" she said.

Gloria's eyebrows rose high. "Oh, really? Like how you're a vegetarian but haven't told Mom and Dad yet?"

"Well—" Lizzie started.

"Or how Dr. Collings always brings you snow globes because one time you told her you collected them? Except you don't collect them anymore, do you? But look at your shelf." Gloria pointed to a shelf on the wall next to her filled with snow globes—only two of which Lizzie had gotten herself. Four years ago.

"It's so nice of her, though . . . ," Lizzie said.

"Or like how you do whatever Sarah says?" Gloria put her sunglasses on again.

Lizzie opened her mouth again and then closed it. Gloria sat back in the chair, looking smug.

"I'm a good friend," Lizzie said finally.

Gloria leaned forward and took off her sunglasses again. "Then be a good sister and tell Mom and Dad that I should have those lessons. Or at least that I should ALSO have those lessons. They listen to you more."

53

Lizzie laughed out loud. The one thing her parents weren't doing lately was listening to her.

She sighed. "Gloria, I don't want the lessons. Mom and Dad said I have to take them to . . ." She wasn't about to give Gloria the satisfaction of hearing that they'd said almost the exact same thing as Gloria. "They said I have to take them, okay? I don't want to. They're making me." Lizzie flopped down on her bed again. She felt her eyes moisten. She'd really had fun with Mr. Samson. But she hated that her parents wouldn't listen to what she wanted.

Gloria was silent so long that Lizzie thought she might have left. Or that something had happened to her. But then she said in a voice that Lizzie hadn't heard for years—her real voice, not the one where she was a dramatic actor—"Do you remember when we used to sing karaoke together?"

Lizzie sat up and looked at her. Gloria had a sweet smile on her face, the way she used to always look before she turned thirteen and became immersed in her "art." Lizzie and Gloria had actually been pretty close—they'd had slumber parties and giggled together. They'd fought, for sure. But when Gloria turned thirteen, Lizzie thought she might actually have become possessed by an alien. An alien that didn't like Lizzie very much.

"Yeah . . . ?" Lizzie said.

"That was fun," Gloria said, standing up. She put her sunglasses back on and threw the boa over her shoulder. Then she said in her normal voice—or what had become her normal voice, anyway—"I should have know that a *baby* couldn't help me. I'll just talk Mom and Dad into it myself." She walked out of the room, leaving Lizzie speechless.

CHAPTER 6
Operation Matchmaker

At seven thirty the next morning, Lizzie opened the door to a fired-up-looking Sarah and a sleepy-eyed Olive and yawning Peter.

"Ready? We have some planning to do!" Sarah practically yelled. She had something clutched to her chest, and her eyes were wide and excited.

Lizzie was dumbfounded. They hadn't really talked about a time, but she sure wasn't expecting anything this early. And she hadn't had a chance to talk to Olive and Peter, either. Everything was happening so fast.

"Um," she said, pulling at her pajama top. "I guess?"

Sarah pushed her way in and tapped the banister three times, then headed to the dining room. Peter shrugged and followed, tapped the banister, and disappeared too. Then Olive, who rolled her eyes and smiled at Lizzie, tapped the banister and joined Sarah and Peter. Lizzie sighed and closed the door. And even though she hadn't just come in, Lizzie also tapped the banister and went into the dining room.

Sarah stood at the end of the big wood farm table, her eyes gleaming. She threw down what she'd been clutching triumphantly.

"Ta-da! Here it is! Our grand plan. Or at least what will hold our grand plan," she said, then sat down with a flop.

Lizzie took a look. On the table was a big binder that had the words OPERATION MATCH-MAKER attached to the front. Olive opened the cover, and Lizzie could see that the papers inside were all blank.

"Today we'll figure out how we're going to get my mom and Sheriff Hadley engaged. They probably just need a little push. So let's sit down and hash this out," Sarah said. She set her mouth, and Lizzie knew she was not in a "let's hear other viewpoints" sort of mood.

A clatter of footsteps came down the stairs and her dad popped into the dining room. "I thought I heard your dulcet tones, Sarah!"

Sarah's brows furrowed. "I don't know what that is, but I'm pretty sure nothing about me is dull."

Olive, Peter, and Lizzie's dad laughed, but Lizzie was with Sarah—she had no idea what that word meant.

"It looks like you're all scheming here," her dad said. "And I think scheming needs pancakes, right?"

All four of them nodded big, and Lizzie's tummy rumbled in response. Her dad grinned and popped into the kitchen, leaving them alone again.

Sarah just looked at them with a huge smile. She raised her eyebrows as if to say "Well?"

Finally, Olive pushed up her glasses and asked, "What is it you want us to do?" She looked as baffled as Lizzie felt.

Lizzie breathed a sigh of relief that Olive had said what she was thinking.

Sarah sighed impatiently. "We need to come up with ideas to get my mom and the sheriff married."

Peter looked around at them, confused. "But . . . I guess I still don't understand why you can't just let them know you know."

Sarah huffed out a breath. "Because it's weird, okay? They didn't tell me for TWO YEARS about them dating. So I feel kind of strange just telling them I know." Something flashed across her face, and Lizzie thought she understood.

Sarah's feelings were hurt.

Lizzie thought about that for a minute. Of course Sarah's feelings were hurt. Lizzie would be really upset if her parents kept something from her for two years. Especially if they did it because they didn't think she could handle it.

And she could understand that Sarah wanted to fight fire with fire—if they hid something from her, she'd hide something from them. Lizzie didn't think this was the best way to handle the whole situation. Not by a long shot. But she understood.

She looked at Olive and saw her struggling with the logic of Sarah's thoughts. But Peter seemed to have understood them the same way Lizzie had, and they shared a look. Olive pressed her lips together for a second. Sarah had stopped talking and was looking down at the table, her face a mixture of anger and hurt. And then Olive got it.

"Okay," Olive said. "I can understand why you want to do it this way. Mostly."

Sarah looked up and smiled. "Mostly is okay, I guess!"

Peter shrugged and glanced at Lizzie. "I'm in if everyone else is."

Lizzie looked at him in shock. Just like that, he was in? They didn't even know what Sarah had in mind! Lizzie needed some time to think. Sarah stared at her expectantly.

It took a second for Lizzie to figure out what she wanted to say. "We—well, um, what is it you're thinking? I think we should know what the plan is. . . ."

Sarah pressed her lips together and said impatiently, "That's what I'm talking about! We need to figure it out."

"But . . . can't you just talk to—" Lizzie said, but Sarah interrupted.

"I'm not doing that, so let's not talk about it."

Her words stung Lizzie. Just like that, Sarah wouldn't even listen to what she had to say. And Lizzie knew deep in her heart that Sarah's plan to trick her mom and the sheriff was not the right way to do anything.

Lizzie was used to this sort of thing from Sarah—though she was getting increasingly irritated with her about it. She looked to Olive and Peter for support.

Olive caught Lizzie's look but shrugged as if to say, "What are you gonna do?" She pushed her glasses up. "The purpose is to get one of them to propose to the other one?"

Sarah nodded and her eyes lit up. "Yes!"

Lizzie tried to catch Olive's or Peter's eyes. Now was the time to say, "Let's figure out a way you can talk to your mom." But no one said anything for a minute.

Lizzie opened her mouth and said, "Maybe a better thing to do—"

But Peter interrupted. "I'm not sure what to do with adults, you know? Like how do we do stuff to make them think a certain way?" He added, "Sorry, Lizzie. I didn't mean to interrupt." He smiled at her and she tried to keep his attention, but it didn't work.

Olive put her finger near her mouth in her thinking pose. "What if . . . What if we practiced on other people first? Get a feel for how to do it?"

Sarah sat up straight. "Like a matchmaking boot camp?"

Olive nodded. Peter slowly smiled and said, "Yeah. That might work."

Lizzie said, "Uh . . ."

Sarah said, "I LOVE THIS IDEA!" She whooped. Her eyes bright, she added, "Lizzie, didn't we see Gloria and her friend Tad talking really close one time? Maybe they should be match . . . maked. Matchmakered. Matchmade. Maybe we should get them together!"

Lizzie shook her head. "I don't think that's a good idea." She thought about her somewhat nice talk with Gloria the day before. It felt a little icky to do this to her.

Olive jumped in. "You know, Peter and I heard our dads talking about Noa and Faiyaz and how they might make a good couple."

Peter said, "I know Noa owns Noa's Grocery Store, but who is Faiyaz again?"

"He's the postman," Olive said.

"Wait—" Lizzie tried to interject.

Sarah said, "Yes, yes. That's perfect. And then there's Stella and Hakeem, of course. I think we all know that Stella is goofy for Hakeem."

Peter and Olive giggled. Lizzie furrowed her eyebrows. "I really don't think this is a good idea—"

But Sarah interrupted. "So, let's start with Tad and Gloria. Let's come up with a plan right now that we'll do next weekend. After that, we'll be matchmakers for Noa and Faiyaz. And then we'll try to get Hakeem and Stella together, finally." She clapped her hands. "I'm so excited! Think of how many people we'll make happy!"

"I don't think . . . ," Lizzie started, but then froze when everyone looked at her. She took a deep breath and said, "Sarah, I'm sorry, but I don't think—"

Sarah put her hand up. "Lizzie, I need you to do this for me. If you're my friend, you'll help." She stared at Lizzie, her brown eyes intense.

Lizzie bit her lip. She just didn't understand why Sarah was so attached to this idea. And it was pretty unfair for Sarah to say something like that about their friendship. But Lizzie took a deep breath and said, "I guess."

There was an awkward silence, and then Olive asked, "So, we'll figure out different ways of getting all of them together, and then choose the best technique to use on your mom and Sheriff Hadley?"

Sarah said, "YES. I think this is the best plan ever. And next weekend we'll put everything into motion. So now we just need to figure out what techniques to use for all three couples."

Right then, Lizzie's dad came out with the pancakes. "Eat up! Everyone knows that eating pancakes helps you make the best schemes!"

Lizzie sighed. She really wished they'd had the pancakes earlier.

CHAPTER 7
Outvoted and Unheard

After her friends had left, Lizzie resolved to do two things. Even though she'd said she'd help Sarah, that didn't mean she couldn't try to prevent some of the damage. She decided she would tell Gloria about their plans—and she'd tell Sarah she'd done it. She wasn't going to lie. But Gloria was her sister and it was only fair. And the second thing was that she would definitely call Olive and Peter to figure out why they were going along with all of this.

Lizzie was experiencing a rare feeling for her: resentment. She resented the fact that she was in this position. And for the first time maybe ever, she felt resentful that it seemed like no one was listening to her.

She walked to Gloria's room and knocked on the door. She hoped Gloria was in one of her good moods, like the last time they'd talked. Lizzie could hear some old movie playing through the door.

Gloria's door opened so fast that Lizzie stumbled back a little. "YES?" Gloria said. She narrowed her eyes when she saw Lizzie. "Oh. It's you. I'm busy." Then she went to shut the door again.

Not in a good mood, evidently.

Lizzie caught the door with her foot. "Wait. Gloria, I have to tell you something."

Gloria snorted. "What could you say that I would possibly be interested in?"

This stopped Lizzie in her tracks. She was used to Gloria's barbs, but this one surprisingly hurt. It was so out of the blue.

"I . . . ," Lizzie started.

"Right. That's what I thought. You have nothing to say." Gloria pushed the door against Lizzie's foot and shut it, leaving Lizzie staring at the wood.

That resentful feeling had turned to anger.

Angry. She was angry!

After their nice talk before, Gloria's mood shift seemed all the more hurtful. But that was the way Gloria was lately—one minute nice, the next minute mean. And yet again, another person who wouldn't listen to what Lizzie had to say.

She hit Gloria's door once with her fist and then recoiled. That hadn't felt really good. Not to her fist and not to her mind. She was so frustrated she started to cry.

Lizzie turned on her heel and went back to her room. She wiped her eyes impatiently. Fine. Gloria deserved any matchmaking they did now. Lizzie had done her duty. And maybe after this, Gloria would finally listen to her.

In her room, Lizzie took deep breaths. Her first task had ended in disaster, she couldn't deny. But as soon as she calmed down a little, a good talk with Olive and Peter would help.

She looked around to see what she could do to get rid of the angry feeling. She saw the speaker dock for her phone. She could sing—no one was listening. And she really did like to sing alone. She put on an old, old song that her parents used to play all the time: "Stand by Me."

At first, she sang pretty softly, but she started to really get into the song and sang a little more loudly, really hitting the "stand by me" chorus. She grinned to herself and started dancing around a little. She twirled and sang, grabbing a hairbrush and singing into it. Even though the last thing she ever wanted to do was sing into a microphone—a device that made your voice LOUDER—she'd seen people do this in movies and it looked like fun. She really let herself go and belted out the song until a knock on the door startled her and she stopped singing abruptly.

"Could you keep it down in there?" Gloria's

voice sounded through the door. "Some of us are trying to watch a movie."

Lizzie sighed and turned down the music. She put the hairbrush down and caught her breath. She normally would have felt really embarrassed, but it was just Gloria. And she was mad at Gloria too. It was kind of freeing.

And anyway, she felt ready to talk to Olive and Peter.

She grabbed her phone and called the number Olive and Peter shared. Olive picked up on the first ring.

"Hey, Lizzie," she said. "Did we forget something at your house?"

Lizzie sat down on her bed and looked out the window. "Hey, Olive. Can you get Peter? I'm wondering if we can talk about something."

Lizzie could imagine Olive pushing her glasses up and looking puzzled. The image made her smile. "Sure," Olive said. "PETER!" she yelled. The sound of footsteps echoed through the phone and then Olive said, "It's Lizzie. She wants to talk."

Peter said, "Is everything okay, Lizzie?"

Lizzie wasn't sure how to start. So she plunged in. "I'm worried about Sarah," she said. When Olive and Peter didn't say anything, she went on. "I don't like calling behind her back, but she won't listen to me." Lizzie choked a little on the last words and the anger swelled up again. She really didn't like to talk about Sarah to people without her knowing—but what choice had Sarah given her?

"It's just . . . I think this plan of hers—of ours—

is not a good idea. Do you guys think it is?" Lizzie stopped talking and bit at a fingernail. This was a lot more nerve-racking than she had thought.

The phone was quiet for a while and then finally Olive said, "Honestly, I don't think it's that big of a deal. Sarah seems to want to do it this way, so I'm okay helping. Besides, what could it hurt? And it will be interesting in a scientific way—to see if pushing people toward each other actually works."

Olive's answer wasn't totally unexpected to Lizzie, even if it was a little disappointing. Olive loved experiments and testing things out. And she wasn't always overly concerned about how other people felt. But Peter was much more like Lizzie, so her next words were directed to him.

"But . . . aren't you worried that . . . isn't it

kind of mean to do experiments on people who aren't, um, volunteering? Like, who aren't aware of what's happening? And don't you think Sarah should just tell her mom what's going on?" Lizzie's heart was racing. She hadn't realized she felt so strongly, but she did. She had known Ms. Shirvani and the sheriff—and everyone in their plans—since forever. It felt really untruthful or sneaky to do this. She added, "And what if it doesn't work?"

Peter said, "Yes, these are good points. I'm worried about it too. I wish Sarah would just tell her mom, but she doesn't want to. And I think she'd go ahead with this plan anyway, so maybe we can help in case anything goes wrong. Plus, what if it goes right? We'll have helped people get together! Sometimes it's hard for people to be brave enough to say their true feelings. And we know these people, or at least you and Sarah do—and they're all really good people so they won't hurt each other."

This quieted Lizzie. She knew Peter was referring to a friend he had had named Kai. It hadn't ended well—Kai had lied about a whole bunch of things and turned out to be someone completely different from what he acted like.

She wasn't sure what to say. It seemed Olive and Peter were on board, and she was the only one who had any reservations.

She felt really alone. And now she also felt like a bad friend for talking about Sarah like this. And also still frustrated that even when someone listened to her, they didn't seem to really hear her concerns.

But she was outnumbered. "Okay. Well, I just wanted to check to see if you're really into this plan," she said, sighing.

"I think it will be totally fine, Lizzie," said Olive.

Peter said, "We'll make sure it doesn't go too far."

Lizzie wasn't sure about either of those things. But she said, "All right. I guess next weekend, we'll be official matchmakers."

CHAPTER 8

Monster Mash of Fun

The next weekend, Lizzie climbed into the car with her dad for her singing lesson. Though she was dreading the lessons less, they were still something she HAD to do, so she wasn't exactly excited. And she still felt pretty down about her sister and her friends. For the first time ever, she felt disconnected from people. And the angry feeling hadn't gone away.

Not to mention, after her singing lesson,

Operation Tad and Gloria was all set to go.

Her dad pulled up to the building and Lizzie jumped out. Her dad said, "Have fun, my little songbird!"

Lizzie smiled a little and walked to the building and into room 128. Mr. Samson sat by the piano, playing a happy tune. He stopped when Lizzie stepped in.

"Well, hello, Ms. Lizzie! How's my favorite Halloween-lover?" he said.

For the first time in a week, Lizzie smiled a big, genuine smile. "I'm fine," she said, taking off her coat and setting it on a nearby chair. She also felt nervous about the possibility of having to sing again, but Mr. Samson was so nice, the nerves really weren't that big this time.

His eyes twinkled. "I have an idea today—I have some Halloween music we can listen to. Want to do that?"

Lizzie brightened. "Yeah! I didn't even know there was Halloween music."

"Oh, yeah! I mean, there are the standards: 'Monster Mash,' 'Werewolves of London,' et cetera. But there are some others that might not be EXACTLY about Halloween but have some scary elements. Should we listen to some songs?"

Lizzie nodded and Mr. Samson went to the far wall and brought out what looked like a CD player. Her parents had one of those, but she didn't even know if it worked.

He plugged it in and put in a CD. "Okay, here's 'Monster Mash.'"

Lizzie giggled. She loved this song. She'd forgotten it even existed.

Halfway through, Mr. Samson started doing a Monster Mash dance. This made Lizzie giggle even harder. He beckoned her over. "Come on, do the Monster Mash!"

Lizzie couldn't help it, she joined in the dancing—after all, she'd just danced in her room, so why not here? Mr. Samson had already been goofy, and she could be too. While they danced, Mr. Samson started singing the low parts. The lyrics said, "He did the Mash," and Mr. Samson would join in, "He did the MONSTER Mash." Lizzie loved his voice.

When the song ended, they were both a

little out of breath and Lizzie felt happier than she had in a long time.

"I have the perfect next song too," Mr. Samson said. He switched CDs and a song that Lizzie had heard before but couldn't remember the name of came on.

"This is 'Thriller' by Michael Jackson. Have you heard this?"

Lizzie nodded. "Yes, but it was a long time ago."

"Well, this one has a complicated dance to it. Want to learn it?" Mr. Samson asked.

Lizzie nodded again. She didn't say it, but she felt like she was learning more about dancing than singing at her singing lesson. But she didn't care. This was way more fun.

Mr. Samson started teaching her the dance. They would take a few steps forward and then put their hands up in the shape of claws and move them from side to side. Lizzie had started giggling again. Mr. Samson started singing the chorus. "Thrilllerrrrr . . . Thriller night."

Before Lizzie even thought about it, she joined in singing the chorus too. Those were the only words she knew, and it was so fun, she couldn't help herself, even if it was in front of someone else.

When the song was over, both Lizzie and Mr. Samson collapsed in laughter.

"That was so fun!" Lizzie said, panting just a little.

"It was! I thought you might like these songs," Mr. Samson said. He changed out the CD and put another one in. "And your voice is just beautiful."

Lizzie started. She hadn't been sure he'd even heard her. But nevertheless, Mr. Samson's words made her feel really good.

The thing was, Lizzie had sort of suspected she had a pretty good voice. She loved to sing alone, and ages ago she even sang karaoke with Gloria. But she'd never even admitted to herself that she had a good voice, let alone said it out loud. The thought of saying that or believing it, and singing in front of people who were staring at her, made her positively quake inside.

The next song Mr. Samson put in was one called "I Want Candy." Lizzie found herself bopping her head along to the beat. Mr. Samson said, "This one doesn't have a dance. But we can dance to it anyway!" So they both moved around and shook their arms and their hips, doing silly moves and laughing. By the end of the song, they were both yell-singing the chorus.

When it was over, Mr. Samson sat at the piano bench and caught his breath. "I'm afraid you're a bit younger than me, my dear. I need to take a break."

Lizzie nodded and sat down too, feeling all the happy energy drain away. She'd forgotten her troubles during the dancing, but now she felt them settle around her shoulders again. Mr. Samson looked at her. "Is there something wrong, Lizzie?"

She frowned and looked down. "I . . . ," she started. Mr. Samson just looked at her, waiting for her to speak.

"Sometimes I feel like my friends don't listen to me. Or my parents. Or my sister," she finally said.

Mr. Samson nodded but didn't say anything.

Lizzie said, "I mean, I'm sorry. Everyone in my life is really nice. But sometimes they just sort of talk over me."

"That's not a good feeling," Mr. Samson said.

"I end up doing things I don't really want to do. I know I should say no, but I can't seem to . . ." Lizzie couldn't find the right words.

"Find the right words?" Mr. Samson said, smiling.

Lizzie sighed and laughed. "Yeah," she said.

"Hmm. Sometimes being the person who sees things or is sensitive can feel lonely."

To her horror, Lizzie felt tears in her eyes. She just nodded.

Mr. Samson slapped his hands on his knees. "Well, I love sensitive people, personally. I myself am one. It can be hard, but that means we can hear the music that no one else can sometimes." He winked at her. "Speaking of, want to hear another song? This one is called 'Zombie.' It's a little different from the others. It's not really a Halloween song, but I thought you might like it. Shall we listen?"

Lizzie sniffed and nodded again and Mr. Samson put the song in. It was different from the others. It was dark and somber, and there were lots of words about fighting and wars in it. Lizzie felt a stirring in her chest when she heard the song—something about it made her feel something big.

"Do you want to try to sing the chorus?" Mr. Samson asked.

Lizzie said, "Yes," right away, without even thinking. Mr. Samson brought out the lyrics. "I'll sing with you to start." He pressed Play on the CD player.

At first, Lizzie felt really self-conscious. But because Mr. Samson was singing too and not looking at her, she loosened up. And the song was so satisfying to sing—she felt it all the way in her gut somehow.

When the song was over, Mr. Samson said, "Wow, Lizzie. That beautiful voice of yours. What a treasure to hear."

Lizzie smiled and swallowed.

"Let's try this again. One thing: try to feel the song right here." He pointed to a place right in the middle of his stomach. "This is the diaphragm. See if you can feel the notes coming from here. It helps you to be heard."

Lizzie nodded, and when the song started again, she really tried to feel the words in her stomach. Sometimes she could, but most of the time she couldn't. Still, Mr. Samson smiled at her with encouragement and they sang the song over and over again.

Before she knew it, the lesson was over. As she put on her coat, she realized her skin was buzzing. Her head felt light and she felt like she'd run a marathon, but she also felt just perfect.

She turned to walk out and then turned

around. "Thank you, Mr. Samson," she said, meaning it with all her heart.

He winked again. "You bet. I'll see you next week, you amazing singer, you."

Lizzie walked out the door smiling.

CHAPTER 9

Operation Tad and Gloria

L ater that day, as she stood outside Gloria's door again, the good feeling Lizzie had had at her singing lesson had all but disappeared. She did not feel prepared for this plan at all.

The phone her parents had gotten her "for emergencies" vibrated in her pocket. She never really liked to use it, but her friends' plan for Tad and Gloria made it necessary. She checked the text message: *Baby bunny is in sight.* This was code for: "We've given Tad the note."

Lizzie sighed. Well. She had a job to do.

She knocked on Gloria's door. "YES?" Gloria said as she threw open the door. She looked at Lizzie "Oh. It's you."

The feeling of déjà vu was overwhelming. Before Gloria could shut the door, however, Lizzie said quickly, "Your friend Tad left this for you," and shoved a bunch of folded papers into Gloria's hands. Then she sprinted away from the door and to her room.

Once she got there, she texted her friends: *The wolf howls at midnight.* The phrase was Sarah's pretty ridiculous idea of a code to let them know she'd handed off the letter.

YES! came the reply. *Come to the shop before Gloria gets here!*

Lizzie flopped on her bed and groaned. She did not want to do this. But Sarah really wanted her there. Lizzie tried to muster enough energy to get up so she could see the whole plan (disaster) unfold.

Tad and Gloria had been best friends since when they were babies. And had even started acting at the same time. Lizzie couldn't remember a time when they weren't hanging out together. Sarah thought they'd be the perfect people to try out their matchmaking skills on. So, even though Lizzie tried to say that Tad and Gloria didn't seem to like each other like that at all—and probably never would—Peter had come up with the idea:

Lizzie would give Gloria a note that said Tad liked her, and to meet him at Annabelle's Antiques to talk about it. And Sarah, Peter, and Olive would find Tad and give him a note that said that Gloria liked him, and to meet her at Annabelle's Antiques.

Which was all well and good, but they couldn't write in Gloria's or Tad's handwriting. But then Olive had the perfect solution: they'd photocopy pages from Shakespeare plays and circle letters that spelled out: "I like you. Meet me outside Annabelle's Antiques." Lizzie couldn't help but think that this was a genius idea, since Tad and Gloria both loved Shakespeare and would totally pass notes like that.

With a grunt, Lizzie got up off the bed, took a deep breath, and ran downstairs. She grabbed her shoes and ran out the door, passing her dad on the way to her bike. "Where are you going, Noodle?" her dad asked.

"To Annabelle's to meet everyone. Is that okay?" Lizzie said, even as she took her bike out and got on it. Her dad knew that "everyone" meant Olive, Peter, and Sarah, and going into town was never a problem. Lizzie was already pedaling when her dad said, "Sure enough!"

It took Lizzie a little while to get into town. The minute she pulled up to the front of the building, she heard, "Psssst!"

Looking around, Lizzie couldn't see anyone. For a second, she thought her bike might have suddenly sprung a leak. But then she heard Sarah whisper loudly, "Lizzie. COME HERE. Hide your bike!"

She saw Sarah's head around the side of Annabelle's and she hurried her bike over, setting it down next to the three already there.

Olive pushed her glasses up and asked, "Any problems?"

Lizzie shrugged. "I don't think so?"

"Did she seem suspicious?" Peter asked.

Lizzie put her hands up in an "I don't know" gesture. "She just seemed like Gloria, that's all."

"So only focused on herself?" Sarah asked.

Lizzie nodded.

"Good. That's good." Sarah looked around the building again. "Holy schmolies, Tad's there!" she whispered in her loud Sarah whisper.

All four of them ducked down and scooted to the end of the wall so they could peer around it. Lizzie hunched over Sarah, who was hunching over Peter and Olive. Sure enough, Tad stood in front of the building, his expression irritated and his feet antsy.

"Uh-oh," Lizzie said, but before she could say anything else, they saw Gloria ride up on her bike, a scarf trailing behind her and her sunglasses huge on her face. She jumped off her bike and said, "Tad. You're here. Give me one moment, darling, while I put my bike down."

Sarah elbowed Lizzie and mouthed, "She said 'darling'!" But Lizzie knew that didn't mean anything. She'd heard Gloria call her meat loaf 'darling' one time.

When Lizzie looked back up, she was horrified to see Gloria heading straight toward them, pushing her bike along. Peter and Olive looked back at Sarah and Lizzie with alarm, and Sarah gestured wildly for them to run around the building. They all scrambled to leave their spots before Gloria saw them. To Lizzie, it sounded like a herd of elephants were stomping away.

The four of them ran around to the other side of the building, where they took up the same positions. Gloria had leaned her bike up against the very corner they had just been at. Lizzie's heart pounded wildly—they'd been so close to getting caught!

Now they could see Tad's back and Gloria walking toward him, an irritated look on her face as well.

When she reached him, Tad said, "What is the meaning of this note?" while at the same time Gloria said, "What is this nonsense, darling? Have you gone mad?"

They both stopped talking and smiled. Tad said, "Did you send me a note to meet me here because you"—he swallowed like he had a bad taste in his mouth—"*like* me?"

Gloria burst out laughing. She laughed so hard, she doubled over, putting her hands on her knees and taking huge, laughing breaths. Tad's smile got bigger and bigger. When Gloria finally calmed down, she said, "Oh, dearest, you do know how funny that is, don't you? And what's even funnier, I received the same note, etched into the works of the bard himself, saying that *you* liked *me*!"

Now both of them doubled over, laughing so hard Lizzie thought one or both of them might pass out. Peter and Olive stood up and looked at Lizzie and Sarah. They looked genuinely confused, all of them, but Lizzie wasn't surprised.

And if her friends had listened to her, they wouldn't have been that surprised either.

Suddenly, Gloria called out, "Come out, babies! We know you're here."

Lizzie closed her eyes and sighed. They were caught. Which meant she could expect Gloria to torture her for the next few weeks.

Without looking at her friends, Lizzie walked around the corner to see Gloria with one elbow on Tad's shoulder and her other hand twirling her scarf. When she saw Lizzie, she pulled down her sunglasses. "I have to admit, you tiny baby, this was a great prank."

Sarah, Peter, and Olive had come out too. Sarah said, "It wasn't a prank—"

But Gloria cut her off with a hand motion. "Surely you didn't think Tad and I would ever possibly *like* each other in that way? Not even you could be that dumb, right?"

Sarah opened and closed her mouth. This was the first time Lizzie had ever heard her speechless.

"I'll give you this—the Shakespeare papers were a nice touch. But the key to a good prank is that it must involve something remotely believable," Tad said. "Gloria is like my sister, Lizzie, you know that. To think of *liking* her is to . . . well, it's to be ridiculous."

Gloria flipped her scarf over her shoulder. "Really, Lizzie, you must have known better."

Lizzie had known better. But no one would

listen to her. She waited for one of her friends to mention that she'd objected to the plan from the beginning, and for this very reason—but instead, Sarah said, "Maybe it's something you just never considered?"

Now Gloria took her sunglasses off and shared a look with Tad. "Oh, darling, you can't be serious. Are you telling me this wasn't a prank? You were just trying to get us together? Oh, no. Oh, that's just tragic."

As the four of them stood there, Tad laughed and grabbed his bike. Gloria grabbed hers. As she got onto the seat, Gloria said, "My dears. Stick to being babies. Matchmaking is just not your thing." And then she rode off, Tad close behind.

None of them said anything for a while. Finally, Sarah shrugged. "Well. Our first try didn't work, huh?"

Lizzie just walked to her bike.

CHAPTER 10

Operation Noa and Faiyaz

Mr. Samson said, "Okay, one more time?"

Lizzie nodded enthusiastically. He gave her a microphone that didn't work but that she used to pretend she was a rock star—just like she did with her hairbrush. With anyone else, she would never even think of doing that, but Mr. Samson was just so much fun.

He pressed Play on "Kill 'Em with Kindness" and began the whistling part in the song. Lizzie grinned. She loved that he had as much fun as she did with these songs. When it was her turn to come in, she put her whole heart into it.

It felt great to just forget everything for a second and concentrate on the song. She belted out the lyrics and danced around the room, getting out of breath.

When the song was over, Mr. Samson said, "Lizzie, say 'A-E-I-O-U' for me."

Lizzie said the vowels.

"Now try not to close your mouth for any of them. Try again."

Lizzie tried again, and she could tell right away that her voice was louder.

"Excellent! Just practice this at home and maybe come in with a song that you really want to sing next week. Sound good?" he asked. He turned around and began straightening things. "Great session today, Lizzie See you next week."

But Lizzie went to get her coat slowly. She felt her feet dragging and couldn't seem to go any faster. The week after the disaster with Gloria and Tad had sped by. And now it was the weekend and she was stuck doing yet another matchmaking try with her friends. Leaving the fun atmosphere of Mr. Samson's music lesson seemed impossible. After a minute, Mr. Samson said, "Everything okay?"

Lizzie thought for a second and then flopped into the nearest chair. "I'm going to go hang out with my friends now," she said. But even she could tell she sounded like she was going to hang out with a firing squad.

"What's going on?" Mr. Samson asked quietly, sitting across from her.

Lizzie shrugged. "Sarah is convinced that we should do this matchmaking stuff. But . . ."

After a second, Mr. Samson said, "But you don't think it's a good idea."

She nodded.

"Can you tell them how you feel?" Mr. Samson asked.

Lizzie looked at her feet. "I tried, but . . . they don't really listen to me sometimes."

"That sounds really frustrating."

She nodded again. But then she suddenly felt like a really bad friend. Here she was complaining about her three best friends in the world. What kind of a friend did that?

She sat up. "Never mind, Mr. Samson. I'm just being silly. I'll see you next week." She stood up and went to the door.

Before she opened it, Mr. Samson said, "Your feelings are important, Lizzie. And so is your voice. Just keep that in mind."

Lizzie smiled and walked out the door, trying to get excited about spending time with her best friends.

Operation Noa and Faiyaz was on track. Or at least as on track as it could be. Sarah went over the details one more time.

"So, we'll go downtown and wait for Faiyaz to start delivering the mail. Then me and Olive will talk loudly about Noa. And then Lizzie and Peter, you pretend to be walking toward him to see his expressions."

Lizzie chewed her lip and a squeak came out.

"Yes?" Sarah said. Already that was unusual—normally Sarah knew exactly what Lizzie's squeaks were about.

For a second, Lizzie wasn't sure how to put her thoughts into words. Then she figured it out. "How do we know for sure that either of them is looking for a boyfriend? And then how do we know that neither of them has a boyfriend already?"

Sarah rolled her eyes, which immediately hurt Lizzie's feelings. Peter noticed and said, "Sarah . . ."

She huffed. "I don't know why you're being difficult, Lizzie."

Olive said, pushing her glasses up, "At the library, Sarah's mom heard Faiyaz talking about being lonely, remember?"

Sarah finished, "And Noa is never with anyone, so he must be single."

Olive said, "So it's a pretty reasonable hypothesis to think they would want to get together."

Peter said, "They just might need a little push. Maybe they're just too shy."

Lizzie still felt uncomfortable. She sighed. "What if they like being by themselves?" Right now, Lizzie wouldn't have minded being by herself.

"Then they don't have to get together," Sarah said patiently. Well, patiently for Sarah, anyway. Mostly she just looked annoyed.

"I guess . . . ," Lizzie said. She didn't want

to be difficult. But she felt exactly the same way she did about Tad and Gloria—this just wasn't a good idea.

"Let's go. Faiyaz delivers the mail around two o'clock," Sarah said. She seemed to be so mad at Lizzie all of a sudden. And Lizzie wasn't sure what to do. She felt lost.

They all grabbed their bikes and started the ride downtown. Lizzie breathed in the cool air and heard the *shoosh*ing of the slush as they rode through the sloppy streets. The winter had been pretty warm, so they could still ride their bikes. This made Lizzie happy, and she was thinking about it when Sarah slowed down to ride beside her and said, "Lizzie, what's going on with you?"

Lizzie was startled. What was going on with

her? She wanted to know what was going on with Sarah! She wasn't the one acting crazy. Before she could say anything, Sarah said, "I just wish you'd be supportive," and then she rode ahead until they reached the hardware store right across from the post office at the beginning of the downtown. They all got off their bikes and leaned them up against the side of the store.

Lizzie felt tears in her eyes. But to her surprise, they weren't tears of sadness—they were tears of frustration. She realized she was . . . upset. She hardly ever got upset, really. But she felt that way now.

Still, because she WAS a good friend, she would participate in the very bad idea that Sarah had. She couldn't look Sarah in the eye, though. Not right at that moment.

They saw Faiyaz come out of the post office right on schedule. Sarah's eyes lit up. "Okay, it's time."

Lizzie didn't say anything and started walking up the street. Peter followed her. They went all the way to Noa's grocery store and watched as Faiyaz started down the street, followed by Sarah and Olive.

Peter whispered to Lizzie as they walked. "Are you okay?"

Lizzie shook her head. "Not really," she whispered back.

"I know this is weird . . . ," Peter said.

Lizzie huffed. "It's not weird. It's just . . . we shouldn't be doing this! And I don't really get why you and Olive want to." She almost stopped walking. This was the most adamant she'd ever been.

When she looked at Peter, his eyebrows were up in surprise.

"Don't you think this is a little fun? We could get Noa and Faiyaz together! What if we make them really happy?" Peter said, gesturing.

They were coming up on Faiyaz, and Lizzie realized they should be looking at his expression. But she whispered back, "What if we hurt someone?" Of all the people in her friend group, Peter was the one to understand that.

But instead, he frowned. "I think that's really negative. And my dad says that the way you think can influence things." Then he went silent.

Lizzie felt tears again. She clearly wasn't getting anywhere. So she changed the subject. "What are they going to say to him again?" she asked.

Peter's frown went away and he smiled. "Not

to him. Behind him. Sarah is going to talk about how Noa mentioned he had a crush on someone with blue shorts who carried a lot of mail."

The tension Lizzie felt eased a little and she laughed just a bit. That was so obvious, there was no way Faiyaz wouldn't know this was a setup. But as they got closer to Faiyaz, both Peter and Lizzie saw Faiyaz's face change. He started walking more slowly, and then his face went from puzzled to surprised to incredibly happy. Lizzie's palms got sweaty. Maybe she had been wrong. Maybe this could actually work! For the first time, she felt a *ping* of excitement.

She and Peter passed Faiyaz and joined Sarah and Olive, and all four of them stopped walking.

"Well?" Sarah asked, excited.

Peter and Lizzie exchanged looks. "He really does look happy about that," said Lizzie. Sarah's face changed and she smiled at Lizzie, like she was finally happy with her again. "That's fantastic!"

Olive asked, "How do we find out if this worked?"

Peter pointed down the road to the entrance of Noa's grocery store, where Lizzie and he had just been. Faiyaz stood outside the door, taking big breaths and looking like he was planning on doing something hard.

All four of them exchanged looks. Then they walked-ran to the grocery store just as Faiyaz walked in.

They watched as he went up to the customer service desk, where Noa stood doing paperwork. The store was fairly empty, so Lizzie and her friends walked to the nearest aisle that was close to the desk but where they wouldn't be seen. They pretended to look at stuff while they listened in. Lizzie got another *ping* of excitement—she had to admit that if this worked, it would feel pretty good. Maybe she should just ignore the little voice that told her it was a bad idea.

Faiyaz said, "Hel-I."

Lizzie felt her face scrunch up in confusion. Then Faiyaz said, "I mean hello. I tried to say 'hi' and 'hello' at the same time." Then he laughed too loudly, and next to her Peter cringed. A feeling of dread crept through Lizzie.

Noa said in a big, booming voice, "Hey

there, Faiyaz. You have some mail for me, do you?"

The four of them peeked around the corner.

Faiyaz shifted on his feet and put his hand in his mailbag. Lizzie saw his hand shaking as he brought a bundle of mail out. He said, "Yeah, just here to deliver stuff to you. Sometimes you don't really know what you have until it's standing right in front of you."

Noa looked up from what he was doing, his eyebrows furrowed. "True, I guess." His voice was much lower.

Faiyaz looked at the floor and then cleared his throat. "Uh . . . so. Well," he said. Noa continued to stare, his face a mask of confusion.

"Do you . . . I think . . . Should we . . . go get

dinner sometime, maybe?" Faiyaz said, his voice squeaking.

Noa swallowed and his face changed from confused to embarrassed to uncomfortable in the space of three seconds. "Oh, Faiyaz," he said softly. "I'm so sorry, but I have a boyfriend in New York."

Lizzie saw Faiyaz close his eyes and let out a breath. "Oh, man. *I'm* the one who's sorry. I thought . . . I heard someone . . . Never mind. Here's your mail!" Then he put the bundle of mail on the counter and practically ran out of the store.

Lizzie, Peter, Olive, and Sarah snapped back around the corner into the aisle. Olive's eyes were squeezed tight, Peter had his hand on his forehead, and Sarah stood with her hands on her hips, looking frustrated. Lizzie realized she was clutching her heart.

Without a word, she turned and walked out the door.

CHAPTER 11
Third Time's the Charm?

izzie, wait up!" Sarah yelled.

With a sigh, Lizzie slowed down and waited for her friends. She was so heartbroken for Faiyaz. And so embarrassed that she'd had any part in this.

When everyone caught up to her, Sarah said, "Well, okay. That one didn't work." Everyone gave her a hard stare.

"I know, I know," Sarah said. "I feel really bad

about this too. But that doesn't mean we should stop trying. We still have one more technique to try on one more couple."

Lizzie could hardly believe her ears. After failing twice—and failing so spectacularly—she couldn't believe Sarah would think it was a good idea to keep going. Lizzie was about to take a big breath to say what she really thought for once, when Sarah's eyes lit up as she looked behind Lizzie. "It's Hakeem," she loud-whispered. "Let's do the last technique now!"

Peter and Olive shared a look. Peter said, "Sarah, I think we've done enough for today."

Lizzie breathed a sigh of relief. Finally. Finally, she wasn't alone in this.

Olive chimed in, "I agree."

Lizzie said, "Maybe now you could go tell your

mom . . . ," but she stopped short at the look in Sarah's eyes.

"I can't believe you guys are going to abandon me," Sarah said. Lizzie couldn't believe it, but she looked sad.

Lizzie shook her head. "We would never abandon you!" she said.

Sarah shrugged. "It feels like it. None of you knows how this feels. You have a perfect dad, Lizzie. And Peter and Olive, you have TWO perfect dads. I don't have ANY. I've never cared, really—not at all. But now that I could have the sheriff as a dad . . . I really want it to happen! Lizzie, I always thought you would support me no matter what. I thought you were a good friend."

Sarah walked away, her head drooping. Lizzie's heart was about to break. She couldn't believe she hadn't thought harder about WHY Sarah wanted these schemes to work so much.

She *was* a bad friend.

A little voice poked at her in her misery. She quieted herself a bit and listened to it. Mr. Samson had said her feelings mattered. And something about this still didn't seem quite right.

She really wished she had known this was how Sarah felt. But . . . messing with other people's lives wasn't the best way to go about getting what she wanted. Faiyaz's face flashed in Lizzie's mind—no, this was definitely not the right way. And wasn't being a good friend saying things friends might not want to hear?

Her heart racing, she opened her mouth to say something, but Olive started talking. She pushed her glasses up and shifted on her feet. "I guess in an experiment, you don't stop after a couple of tries," she said, putting her hand on Sarah's. Sarah gave her a grateful look.

Peter looked at Lizzie just briefly but then said, "Yeah. I guess we'd be quitters if we let a couple of fails stop us. And anyway, maybe we still have a chance to make people happy." Then he looked at Lizzie pointedly. "To make a few people happy."

Sarah grinned, and Lizzie felt the weight of all their stares. That little niggling feeling was poking at her still. But the look on Sarah's face and her echoing words started to wear her down. If she was the only one in their way, maybe she *was* being a bad friend.

She said quietly, "Okay."

Sarah whooped and pumped her fist in the

air. "I have the best friends ever!" she practically yelled. Lizzie wasn't so sure. Sarah turned her head toward the place where Hakeem had been, but it looked like he had gone into his store already.

Sarah said, "Okay, Operation Stella and Hakeem is a go. Let's get to the store now—it looks pretty empty."

Without waiting for an answer, Sarah strode past all of them and went straight to Hakeem's door. Peter looked at Lizzie and shrugged, as if to say "Here we go again," and Lizzie managed a weak smile. She knew that Olive and Peter were doing this now to make Sarah feel better. And Lizzie wanted her to feel better too. But she sure wasn't going to muster any enthusiasm.

Sarah opened the door and the bell chimed.

Hakeem's familiar voice reached them. "Well, look! My favorite kids are right here inside my store." Lizzie smiled with the rest of her friends. It was impossible not to smile around Hakeem. "What brings you into the store today? What can I help you with?"

For the first time during all her ideas, Sarah looked a little uncertain. But then she blurted out, "We think Stella likes you."

Lizzie squeaked. She saw Peter's eyes go wide and Olive shake her head and look down. Lizzie closed her eyes. Sarah said, "I mean, we think you and Stella might make a . . . might be a good . . ." She stopped talking and the store got really quiet. Lizzie opened her eyes and peeked at Hakeem, an equal mix of dread and hope battling within her.

Hakeem's expression was kind but sad. He patted Sarah on the shoulder. "Oh, my dear. Stella is a wonderful lady. But my heart has only ever belonged to one."

Lizzie felt tears spring to her eyes. She thought she knew who he was talking about. She cleared her throat. "Your wife?" she asked softly.

Hakeem nodded sadly. "Yes. It's been ten years now since she passed. But a day doesn't go by that I don't talk to her. She is always here." He pointed to his heart. Then he pointed to the shrine he had to her in the store. "And there. We have entire conversations. Until I can meet her again, this is how we communicate."

Sarah sighed. "I'm sorry, Hakeem." Lizzie did a double take. Sarah wasn't the best apologizer. But even she felt bad now. Maybe she could see that all this meddling was hurtful. Hurtful and . . . for the first time, Lizzie thought the word: selfish. Immediately she felt like a bad friend. She banished the thought from her head.

Suddenly Hakeem laughed. "Now look! You were all trying to do something nice for me and I made you sad. Nonsense! Who can be sad when we live in New Amity? When we have friends galore and good food and beautiful weather? Not me! You sweethearts don't feel bad for a minute!" He gave each of them a big hug. Then he took out four big jawbreakers and handed one to each of them. "Now, go play and have fun and don't think for one more second about an old man and his happiness. You have better things to do! Go!" He shooed them out of his store, pretending to use a flyswatter. All four of them were giggling by the time they stepped onto the sidewalk. Their cheeks bulged with the jawbreakers.

Once they were on the sidewalk, their giggles died down and their smiles disappeared. Everyone was quiet for a moment. And then Olive said, "I think we should go back to the orchard."

Lizzie nodded. Yes. Maybe they could all talk. They could make Sarah feel better AND convince her not to go ahead with the next part of her scheme—the actual matchmaking between the sheriff and Ms. Shirvani. If all of their practice runs had gone so horribly wrong, well . . . how would it be when they did the one they wanted to do for real! It was time for a plan B. Lizzie felt a huge weight lift off her shoulders. Surely this would mean no more matchmaking. She was really glad Sarah had been truthful with them, even if it had hurt her feelings. Maybe she could convince Sarah to do the same with her mom. There was a little hope, anyway.

The four of them walked to their bikes and then rode side by side, silent, all the way back to the orchard.

CHAPTER 12

End Game

When they got back to the orchard, they dropped their bikes in the yard and walked into the house, tapping the banister three times. Then they went to the living room and settled in. Lizzie snuggled into her favorite chair, ready to console Sarah and come up with a plan B.

Sarah flopped onto the couch and looked at Peter and Olive, who had found two of their favorite squishy chairs and snuggled in too. Then she looked at Lizzie.

And a gigantic grin broke out over her face. "Well, I think we can say that was a HUGE success, right?" She beamed and looked at each of them in turn.

Lizzie squeaked.

"Um . . . ," Olive said.

Peter said, "How now?"

What was happening? After her big confession, the terrible time with Faiyaz and Noa . . . after Hakeem's story and even the scorn from Tad and Gloria, Sarah somehow thought it was a success?

Sarah wiggled on the couch and leaned forward. "Okay, it's true that our matchmaking didn't work. But our TECHNIQUES did."

Olive scrunched up her face and pushed her glasses up. "What, now? If our techniques had worked, we would have gotten the outcomes we wanted, Sarah. That's how experiments work."

Sarah shook her head. "Well, that's *one* way to know if something worked. But think about this: Tad and Gloria *did* meet—which is what we wanted them to do. And Faiyaz *did* ask Noa out, which is what we wanted him to do. And Hakeem totally talked to us about Stella and . . . everything. None of it worked *exactly* just because none of them *wanted* to actually be together. But my mom and the sheriff *do*."

She sat back triumphantly.

Lizzie shook her head. This was not what she'd expected. Sarah just saw and heard what she wanted to see and hear.

Lizzie looked at Olive and Peter. Olive spoke. "I guess there's some logic there. It's true—they did what we wanted them to do. It just wasn't the outcome we'd hoped for. . . ."

Peter said, "And your mom and Sheriff Hadley are already together. . . . Getting them to propose means just a little push."

Lizzie shook her head. She squeaked. "But . . . ," she said.

Sarah looked at her, her eyes wary. This broke Lizzie's heart yet again. She could see that Sarah was ready to argue with her.

Lizzie took a deep breath. She HAD to say this. "You could still just tell your mom, right?"

Sarah rolled her eyes and glared. "We already talked about that, Lizzie. What's the point in

bringing it up again? I think we have to concentrate on putting these plans in motion. Do you
want to help or not?"

Lizzie looked away. She didn't want to help.
But she didn't want to not help. She didn't say
anything.

"You're in, then," Sarah said, not waiting for
an answer from Lizzie. "Which is good, because
I think for the first technique, you should be
the one who hides the note. You're always at the
library . . . you can hide a note for my mom in one
of the books, no problem." She stared at Lizzie
hard. Lizzie looked away, then nodded.

Olive jumped in, easing the tension a little.
"We have a problem, though. We can't use a
Shakespeare play this time."

Peter added, "True. That's a good point, Olive. What would be something Sheriff Hadley would like?"

Sarah sat back, her mouth twisted and her eyebrows furrowed. "I don't know. I don't really pay any attention to what grown-ups like. . . ."

Lizzie had an idea that could work. But she really didn't want to say it. She truly hated this idea—but Sarah was getting madder and madder at her, it seemed. And she was on the verge of thinking Lizzie wasn't a good friend. The thought of that made Lizzie cringe—she was always a good friend. It was what she did. She swallowed down her own feelings and cleared her throat. She said, "We can use a script from *Doctor Who*. Your mom likes *Doctor Who* too, so it makes sense. Also, the sheriff writes in block letters, so we don't really have to worry about it if we try to write like him."

Sarah's eyes got wide and she bounced on the couch. "Lizzie you're a genius!" And now she looked at Lizzie with happy eyes.

Lizzie smiled, but she knew it wasn't one of her big smiles. Sarah didn't notice.

"This is great. Okay, let's work on the note now. And then I think we have to help Mr. and Mrs. Garrison with the decorations for the dance again. But then tomorrow . . . we'll go to the library and try it out!" Sarah said.

Peter and Olive nodded and Lizzie did too. But mostly she was thinking: *I wish I were still at singing practice.* A thought that surprised even her.

CHAPTER 13
The Chase

Lizzie stood behind a bookshelf, peeking out to watch Ms. Shirvani. Ms. Shirvani talked animatedly near the children's section to a little girl who held a teddy bear. The little girl looked confused.

Near Ms. Shirvani, Lizzie could see a boy who looked to be around five years old poking an older kid near him who was reading a book. "I'm BORED," the kid said loudly. The older kid poked him back and said, "Stop it, Ethan. I want to finish this book." He went back to reading. Lizzie knew immediately they were brothers. She was pretty sure this same thing had happened between Gloria and her. Only the other way around. Ethan sighed and walked around the children's area, touching every book on the shelf.

Lizzie swallowed and took the papers out of her pocket. They were a *Doctor Who* script that she and her friends had turned into a love note for Ms. Shirvani from the sheriff. She looked at the circled letters and closed her eyes. Her gut told her this would work about as well as their other match-making tries. Meaning—not at all. But she'd promised she'd help. The letters they'd circled said, "We should talk about . . ." and then Lizzie had written in block letters: "getting married. Love, Colin."

The four of them had argued about what to put on the note. The problem was, they didn't want to actually propose to Ms. Shirvani for the sheriff. They just wanted her to know it was coming. And then it took them a while to remember what Sheriff Hadley's first name was. But finally they'd agreed on what to say. Now Lizzie stood behind a stack of books, trying to figure out a way to get the note to Ms. Shirvani.

After thinking of a hundred different ways to do it, Lizzie finally realized: there was nothing to do but try to place it on her desk. Which was hard because her desk was right in the open. Lizzie glanced at Ms. Shirvani talking to the little girl. She seemed pretty absorbed in the conversation, even if the little girl wasn't. But that was good— Ms. Shirvani tended not to notice things around her when she was really involved with something. Very much like her daughter.

Lizzie took a deep breath, closed her eyes briefly, then walked as quickly as she could to the main desk. Once she was there, she looked around for a place to tuck the papers so that it was obvious enough to catch Ms. Shirvani's attention. But suddenly, she heard Ms. Shirvani say, "Let me go to my computer to see if we have that book, Chloe."

Lizzie's heart dropped into her stomach. She quickly threw the papers on the desk, right out in the open, then ran-walked back to the stacks. She slipped behind the same bookcase she'd just been hiding behind and peeked around the corner. Her heart felt like it was going to gallop out of her chest.

Ms. Shirvani had been making a beeline for the desk, but then she suddenly stopped. "Chloe, follow me. I know exactly where that book is." She turned on her heel and strode back to the little girl. Lizzie breathed a sigh of relief. She could hide the note better now. Otherwise, she had a feeling Ms. Shirvani would search the library for whoever had left it. Sneaking out while she was on high alert would be next to impossible.

Lizzie walked back toward the desk, but the little boy, Ethan, got there first. He idly touched all the things on the desk, including the note. Not only did he touch it, but to Lizzie's horror, he picked it up.

Lizzie hurried over to the boy, checking to make sure Ms. Shirvani was nowhere to be seen.

She reached the desk and whispered to Ethan, "Hey, can I have those?"

The boy immediately narrowed his eyes and pulled the papers to his chest. "No. Why? What are they? Are they a treasure?"

Lizzie looked behind her and saw that Ms. Shirvani was still occupied. But she didn't know how long that might last. So she leaned in and said, "Listen. I would really, really appreciate it if you could just give them to me. They're not a treasure. I promise."

The boy smiled a naughty smile. "Why do you want them so bad?"

Lizzie was dumbfounded. "I . . . I just do. Just give them back."

The boy clutched the papers harder. Then he broke out into a huge grin. "I'll give you the papers if you catch me!" he said. And then, to Lizzie's continuing horror, he raced right toward the library door.

Lizzie ran after him, not even checking to see if Ms. Shirvani had seen her. As the boy burst out of the door, he ran past Sarah, Olive, and Peter, who had been standing outside, waiting. Lizzie ran past them too and squeaked out, "He's got the note!"

Now all four of the friends chased the little boy. Lizzie could hear Ethan giggling the entire time, and she was starting to lose steam. Sarah passed her, and then Olive and Peter did too. The boy ran around the building and veered off to some nearby trees. All four of them caught up to him, Lizzie breathing so hard she thought she might pass out.

The boy hid behind a tree, giggling. Sarah lunged for him, but he ran around the tree with Sarah chasing him. Peter stepped in front of the boy, Sarah to the side, and Lizzie and Olive stepped in front. They finally had him surrounded.

They all leaned over and caught their breath. Lizzie leaned a little on Olive, who leaned back. The boy guffawed—he was definitely not bored anymore.

Sarah said, breathing hard, "Little kid . . . give us . . . the papers."

He said, "Okay." Then he laughed and threw the papers in the air. "CATCH!" he yelled, and barreled right between Lizzie and Olive and ran away.

As the boy ran away, all four of them tried

to catch the papers coming down. A breeze had started and carried a couple of the papers away. Finally, they managed to gather them all, and they ended up in Lizzie's hands again.

"All right! Let's try again," Sarah said. Lizzie groaned.

CHAPTER 14

A Slippery Slope

This time around, Sarah, Olive, and Peter made some loud noises outside the library to distract Ms. Shirvani. Lizzie slipped in and managed to place the papers in her datebook, which Sarah thought was genius. She knew her mom would absolutely see them, since she called her datebook her "brain." Lizzie's heart almost jumped out of her chest during the whole ordeal. She was so done with sneaking around. But she gathered her strength for the next part of their plan: Sheriff Hadley. Which involved finding him.

Lizzie met Peter, Sarah, and Olive outside the library and they walked farther into town on Main Street. The police station was a place Lizzie and Sarah had gone many times before to see Sheriff Hadley. Walking there took hardly any time, and Lizzie could do it in her sleep. She really did understand why Sarah wanted Sheriff Hadley as a stepdad. He was funny and kind, and he loved goofing around with Sarah. She had to admit, if anyone could be a good stepdad to Sarah, it was Sheriff Hadley. She had a momentary pang of happiness for her friend—even though all these schemes were making her crazy.

On the way there, Olive asked, "Lizzie, how are the singing lessons? You didn't want to take them, right? Can you get out of them?"

Lizzie smiled a little. "Actually . . . ," she said.

Sarah piped up. "I've heard you sing, Lizzie. You really do have a good voice."

Lizzie blushed. "Thanks. It's more that I like my teacher. He's really . . . different."

"Different how?" Peter asked.

Lizzie was so glad they'd asked—she'd wanted to tell them about Mr. Samson for a while. But everything had been about Sarah lately. Lizzie was about to answer but realized they'd already arrived at the police station, and everyone seemed to forget all about her. A part of Lizzie was a little relieved—having all the attention never felt totally good to her. But she also felt bad. If she could have answered the question, she would have said, "He's fun and he really listens to me."

Sarah pressed her face against the door of the station. "He's not here," she said, frowning.

"We know he's not with your mom," Peter pointed out.

Olive pushed up her glasses. "Hmm. Where does he go when he's not in the station?"

Lizzie said, "It's Sunday." But no one heard her.

Olive said, "You know . . . it's Sunday. And it's lunchtime. Maybe he's eating lunch? Probably at home, actually."

Sarah snapped her fingers. "Or Dinah's Diner. Let's check that out! He loves eating there."

Lizzie's stomach growled. Grabbing something to eat might be nice, anyway.

They walked to the diner, and sure enough, the minute they walked in, they heard Sheriff Hadley's voice. They all shared a smile—even

Lizzie. This was some pretty good luck.

Not only that, but the booth in front of the sheriff was empty—a perfect place to carry out part two of their plan.

Sarah whispered, "Peter and Olive, you guys sneak into the kitchen, peek out the door, and watch his face to see his reaction while Lizzie and I talk. Just like we did with Operation Noa and Faiyaz." Lizzie's heart skipped a beat. She really wished she hadn't said that. Operation Noa and Faiyaz had been a disaster. But Sarah went on. "Lizzie and I will sit behind him and say the lines, pretending we don't know he's there."

Olive pushed her glasses up. "How are we going to get into the kitchen without him seeing? He's facing it! Also, won't he see us peeking out?" she whispered.

At that moment, Rachel came out of the kitchen with food and walked to Sheriff Hadley's booth.

"Go!" Sarah whisper-yelled.

Peter and Olive scrambled left and Lizzie and Sarah hurried right. Lizzie slid into the booth as quickly as possible with Sarah just a beat behind.

Lizzie's heartbeat tripped as she thought of this next step. Rachel left the sheriff's table, and Lizzie could hear the sheriff pick up his utensils and start eating his lunch.

Sarah turned to Lizzie with a smile. Lizzie knew that meant Sarah was going to jump into the plan. Lizzie took a deep breath as Sarah said loudly, "Lizzie, did you know my mom is dating someone?"

Lizzie cleared her throat. "No," she squeaked. Sarah elbowed her and she said, "No," more forcefully.

"She sure is!" Sarah said, almost yelling. "Yes, and I think he's the best. It's a secret, though, so I can't tell you who. But I can tell you . . . " Here she paused, Lizzie thought a little dramatically. "I would LOVE for him to be my stepdad."

Lizzie stared at her—this was so bold! But then Sarah elbowed her again and she snapped out of it. "Oh, that's so great!" she said.

Sarah said, "Yeah. I wish he'd ask her to marry him."

A crash from Sheriff Hadley's booth startled both Lizzie and Sarah. And then the sheriff's fork clattered to the floor.

For some reason, this spooked Lizzie and seemed to spook Sarah as well, so they both got up and ran to the kitchen, past the sheriff, who was too busy trying to clean up his mess to notice them.

When they ran through the swinging door, they almost hit Peter and Olive, who had started giggling. This made Lizzie and Sarah giggle too.

"That was so close!" Peter said as he laughed.

Sarah snorted a little. "I can't believe we made it in here without him seeing us! Or figuring out we knew he was there." Her laugh shook her whole body, making Lizzie laugh even harder too.

Sarah wrapped her arms around her stomach and stepped back, still in the throes of her laugh. But to Lizzie's horror, Sarah stepped down on a spoon and suddenly began to slide. Her whole body slid right into a table and she fell down to the floor with a big WHOMP. And as she did that, Sarah's flailing arm knocked a huge bowl of spaghetti right off the table, which promptly upended directly on her head. The crashing hadn't stopped, though—she'd somehow knocked into a row of pans, which banged into each other and clattered so loudly it hurt Lizzie's eardrums.

For a second, no one moved. Then it seemed like everyone moved at once. Lizzie ran to Sarah. Olive and Peter ran to Lizzie. Rachel ran in from the dining room. And then shortly after that . . . Sheriff Hadley stepped into the kitchen.

Rachel said, "Are you okay? What happened?" She ran to where Lizzie and her friends were.

Sarah stood up slowly and took the bowl off her head, long spaghetti strands running down her face. She cleared her throat and put her chin up. She looked at Sheriff Hadley and said, "Hey. My mom wants to marry you."

Then she looked at all her friends, Lizzie last, and said, "RUN!"

CHAPTER 15

The Worst Plan Yet

At Lizzie's house, even as they worked on the decorations for the dance, Sarah still had spots of spaghetti sauce in her hair. Every time Peter, Lizzie, or Olive tried to point it out, Sarah ignored them. So finally, they all gave up and glued hearts and cupids and sprinkled glitter.

Sarah eventually said, "Well, I think we did it. I mean, I guess we won't know until one of them actually proposes, but"—she shrugged and smiled—"I think we got the point across!"

Olive said, pushing up her glasses, "Yeah, I think this plan went off with a BANG." Lizzie, Olive, and Peter giggled.

"You really used your noodle, Sarah," said Peter.

Lizzie added, "Hopefully something will PAN out."

All four of them—even Sarah—collapsed into giggles.

Finally, Peter said, "When do you think they'll do it? Or how? And do you think they will?"

Sarah said, wiping yet more spaghetti sauce off her face, "Of course they will. Why wouldn't they?"

Lizzie stayed quiet. She thought Sarah might just want them to do it and wasn't thinking straight. She wasn't sure at all that the plan had worked. But the idea of being a bad friend again kept her mouth shut.

"I'm not sure when or where they'll do it, but I hope it's soon," Sarah said.

Olive grinned. "What about in a week?" she said.

All three of them looked at her. Sarah said, "Sure . . . ? A week would be fine."

Olive pushed up her glasses, excited. "What if we could provide the perfect, most romantic place? With all the right people there? What if we had the perfect lab conditions for a proposal to happen?" She waved around the heart she was gluing.

"Cool . . . ," Sarah said, still looking confused.

Peter said, "OH!" all of a sudden. He'd clearly understood what Olive was getting at.

And a second later, Lizzie did too. She, Peter, and Olive said at the same time, "The dance!"

Sarah said a second later, "THE DANCE! Oh my gosh, that's perfect! That's the PERFECT place for this to happen. And it's next Saturday!"

Peter's eyes shone. "We could actually get people together! And make them happy! But how do we make sure it happens? I mean, do we give them another note?"

The room was silent as they all thought about it. Lizzie was secretly relieved . . . maybe this would end the whole thing. There was no reason to keep pushing this, no reason at all. And with this stumbling block, the whole ordeal could be over.

Then Sarah's face slowly brightened. "I've got it." She beamed at them. "I know exactly what to do."

"Well?" Olive asked, pushing up her glasses.

"Lizzie," Sarah said.

Lizzie jumped at her name. "What?" she said.

"You," Sarah said.

"Me what?" Lizzie felt unease growing.

"YOU COULD SING! You could sing a song and say beforehand—'This would be a perfect song to propose to someone to!'" Sarah bounced up and down in her seat.

Olive's face broke out in a huge grin. She said, "Yes, these are the exact conditions that would do it. I think this is a good idea."

Peter nodded, smiling big. "This is a GREAT idea," he said. "It's perfectly romantic."

They all looked at Lizzie expectantly.

But Lizzie's head was buzzing like a swarm of angry bees had gotten in. She could hardly talk. Why would they ever think that was something she would want to do? Did they not know her at all? Didn't they know how mean it was even to ask her?

She opened her mouth and then closed it. The answer was no, of course. Of course she didn't want to do that. For many reasons. But she couldn't seem to speak.

"Uhhh . . . ," she said. Though it was more of a sound than a word. Just as she gathered up her courage, the front door opened.

"Kids!" her dad called.

"We're home!" her mother boomed.

"In here," Sarah yelled back. Lizzie still hadn't spoken. Her parents walked in and her mom came up behind her, rubbing her back.

"The decorations are really coming along!" she said, and squeezed Lizzie's shoulder.

"Mr. and Mrs. Garrison. We have the best idea for the dance," Sarah said.

"Yes?" Mr. Garrison asked, smiling.

"Well, you know how my mom and Sheriff Hadley are together, right?" Sarah said.

Lizzie's mom lifted her hand from Lizzie's shoulder, and Lizzie turned around to look at her. Her face was shocked. Her dad's face was too. Had they not known?

"Oh, honey, how do you know?" her mom asked.

Sarah said, "I figured it out."

"Are you okay?" Lizzie's dad asked.

Her mom looked at Lizzie. "OH, so this is what was happening a couple of weeks ago around your first singing lesson." Lizzie nodded.

Sarah grinned. "I'm so happy about it!"

Both of Lizzie's parents smiled relieved smiles. Her mom patted her chest where her heart was. "Oh, I'm so glad to hear that. So glad," she said.

"In fact, I WANT them to get married. And we think the dance would be the perfect place for the proposal to happen," Sarah said. "And . . . even better . . . we think Lizzie should sing at the dance." Her eyes shone, and Lizzie stared at her in disbelief.

She had hope, though. Her mom and dad would SURELY know this wasn't something she would do. This wasn't something she would ever WANT to do EVER.

But the worst thing happened instead.

Her mom looked at her dad and her dad looked at her mom. And then at the same time, her dad WHOOPED and her mom said, "YES! I LOVE this idea!"

Her mom put her hands on Lizzie's shoulders again. "This is such a GREAT idea. Lizzie can show off what she's learned at her singing lessons—her teacher says her voice is lovely—and Colin and Ana can get engaged! It's just a matter of time, really. And I can't think of a better place for it to happen!" she said. "Lizzie, I'll call Mr. Samson and get you in this week to practice whichever song you're going to sing. Sarah, this is a fantastic idea!"

Lizzie shook her head but couldn't speak. She was too close to bursting into tears. She glanced up and saw Gloria in the doorway, frowning. Lizzie shook her head. She was probably mad that Lizzie would have the spotlight.

And Lizzie would do anything to give it to her.

CHAPTER 16

Singing Lessons

Y ou seem really quiet, Lizzie," her dad said as he drove her to her special singing lesson that Wednesday. Lizzie wasn't sure what to say. Of course she was quiet. She'd never felt quite so alone. She thought that if one of her friends had felt this way, or even one of her parents, she'd have known exactly what was going on. But it seemed like no one listened to her OR understood her.

She'd spent the past two days avoiding everyone. And it hurt her deeply that Sarah hadn't even come to check on her. She'd only sent a text to her: *Sing Cant help falling in love.* She hadn't asked Lizzie once how she felt.

No one had.

"You must be a little nervous about the dance. Of course you are. Well, Mr. Samson will help with everything—Mom says you like him?" her dad asked.

This Lizzie could talk about. "Yeah. He's pretty cool," she said, her voice still low. She didn't say anything else, and her dad pulled into the parking lot just a few minutes later.

When she got into the room with Mr. Samson, he could tell right away that something was wrong. She took one look at his face and started crying.

He led her over to a chair and sat her down, then handed her a bunch of Kleenex.

After a few minutes of crying and hiccupping, Lizzie calmed down and said, "Thanks."

Mr. Samson said, "Do you want to talk about it?"

Lizzie hesitated, then nodded. "My friends want me to sing a song at the dance on Saturday so that Sarah's mom and Sheriff Hadley will get married," she said.

Mr. Samson looked confused, but Lizzie didn't even know where to start with Sarah's crazy plans. So she just said, "But I don't want to." She started to cry again. "And no one asked me if I wanted to. Not even my parents. Not even Sarah. It's like it doesn't matter what I want or what I say at all," she said.

She wiped her eyes and Mr. Samson nodded. "That sounds awful," he said.

"I know I should stop complaining," Lizzie said as a stab of guilt poked at her. She was being disloyal to her friends.

Mr. Samson said gently, "Well, I understand why you feel that way. But I'm wondering if that's the real solution here? To stop 'complaining'?"

Lizzie looked up. "What is the solution?"

"I'm just wondering, Lizzie, what would happen if you told them how you feel? If you spoke up?" he said.

She twisted her mouth and thought about that. She had almost said the exact same thing to Sarah. But it felt impossible, even though she didn't know why. She shrugged at Mr. Samson.

He looked at her intently for a moment while she stayed silent, then slapped his hands on his knees. "Okay, then. Well, we should practice if you're going to sing the song on Saturday, huh?" Lizzie's stomach dropped. She took a deep breath and nodded. Mr. Samson asked, "What song are you going to sing?"

"Sarah said 'Can't Help Falling in Love.'"

Mr. Samson said, "Got it. I am positive I have this song in there somewhere. It's pretty popular." He shuffled through some sheet music and after a minute said, "Aha!" Then he pulled it out and handed it to Lizzie. "I'll play the piano here and you can sing along, okay?" Lizzie nodded again and Mr. Samson said, "And maybe try not to look so miserable?" He smiled a nice smile at her and she couldn't help smiling back.

They practiced for a while until Lizzie had memorized the words, which didn't take too long. But still, her heart wasn't in it, and it wasn't her favorite song, so the lesson seemed to last forever. With about ten minutes left in the lesson, Mr. Samson said, "Let's talk about a strategy for the dance, okay?"

Lizzie set down the music and waited.

"First," Mr. Samson said, "you'll want to try to practice with the band a couple of times during the day so you know how to work together."

This surprised Lizzie and made her nerves fizz all over again. That meant she would be singing in front of people a few times. It made sense, now that she thought of it, but it just hadn't occurred to her.

"Second," Mr. Samson said. Then he sighed. "You have another option. An option that would mean you don't need to sing at all, if you don't want to."

Lizzie perked up. She liked the sound of this.

"Just like we talked about, you can tell them no," Mr. Samson said, then gave her a meaningful look.

Lizzie looked down and looked up. "I don't think I can, Mr. Samson," she whispered.

He nodded. "I understand. But know that if you decide to do that, it's okay. Just to be clear: your feelings and thoughts are just as important as everyone else's." Then he piled up the music papers and handed them to her. "But if you're going to go ahead and sing, just practice in your room, and then ask to see the band before the dance to practice. And you'll be just fine. You have a beautiful voice, Lizzie. And it would be fantastic if others heard how beautiful it is. But that's always your choice. Always." He stood up and Lizzie did too. He gave her an encouraging smile and led her to the door.

"Always your choice," he said as she walked out. Lizzie knew he was right, but it sure didn't feel like it.

CHAPTER 17
The Dance

The barn bustled with people making last-minute preparations. Hakeem hung hearts on one wall while Gloria and Sheriff Hadley set up the punch table in the corner. Noa swept the floor and Stella told people where to put things. Lizzie's mom and dad ran back and forth, carrying food, drinks, decorations, and all manner of dance-related things. In only one hour, the dance would start and Lizzie would be forced to sing in front of everyone.

Her entire body hurt. Her throat was tight. Her heart was pounding. And she'd put her dress on backward three different times. When she looked down at her feet, she was wearing one navy blue and one black ballet flat. It was hard to tell the difference in the light of the barn, but it made her all the more nervous. She stood in the corner, nervously biting her fingernails.

She'd been avoiding everyone, especially the band. She was supposed to practice with them, she knew, but even the thought of doing that made her knees shake. Every time her parents asked about it, she found a way to run away. As she sat there thinking about that, she wondered why she was in the barn at all. People were starting to look at her.

She stopped chewing her fingernail and walked quickly to the barn door. But Aaron, Rachel's husband and a band member, stopped her.

"Hey, Lizzie! We've been looking for you. Do you want to practice the song?" He leaned in and said, "I love the idea of encouraging people to propose!"

Lizzie was horrified. She hadn't realized the band was in on it. But of course they were—her parents were probably the ones who had clued them in. She swallowed. "Is it . . . do you think we could . . . not practice?" she said, whispering.

Aaron's eyebrows furrowed. "Well . . . I guess?" he said. "I'm not sure that's a great idea, though."

But Lizzie said, "Great, thanks!" and walked away as quickly as possible. She walked away so quickly that she didn't even pay attention to where she was going and walked smack into Sarah.

"LIZZIE!" Sarah yelled. "THERE you are! We've been looking for you." Olive and Peter stood behind her. Peter looked intently at Lizzie. She looked away from him and mumbled, "Yep, I'm here. But I have to go . . . over there." She turned and walked to the punch bowl, where the sheriff and Rachel were setting up the cups.

"Oh, look. The *baby* is here," Gloria said. Rachel smiled and moved away and suddenly Gloria turned to Lizzie.

"What are you doing?" Gloria asked, not in her usual "acting" voice.

"I—uh . . . uh . . . ," Lizzie stammered.

"I-uh," Gloria mimicked her impatiently. "You clearly don't want to sing tonight, so why are you going to do it?"

Lizzie was so shocked she couldn't even open her mouth. Gloria sighed. "Look, this sort of thing makes you miserable. Mom and Dad are pretty clueless. So YOU have to speak up, you know. People can't read your mind."

"Hey, Lizzie and Gloria," Sheriff Hadley said as he came to stand by them. Gloria cleared her throat and said in her normal "acting" voice, "Babies should listen to their elders." She gave Lizzie a meaningful look and floated away.

Sheriff Hadley said, "Bye, Gloria." He turned to Lizzie, who was still reeling from her sister's words. "How great is this dance, huh? I hear you and your friends have done a lot to contribute. Albert and Tabitha say the four of you have been scheming away!"

Before Lizzie could say anything, Ms. Shirvani

walked up to the sheriff and gave him a smile that Lizzie couldn't quite read. "Hi, Colin," she said, but her eyes were troubled. Then she turned to Lizzie. "Oh, hi, honey! Sarah is coming over right now," she said. "I went to talk to her but she said she needed to follow you because you're 'weird' or something? I didn't quite hear her, to be honest, love."

Lizzie looked up to see Sarah walking toward her purposefully, but right then, the band started playing and people began arriving for the dance. Someone intercepted Sarah, and while she talked to them, Lizzie ducked away. If she could just avoid everyone for the whole dance, she wouldn't have to sing. Plus, so much was happening all at once, she couldn't seem to catch her breath.

More and more people came in, which helped hide Lizzie from Sarah or anyone else who might be confusing and demanding. Lizzie wove in and out of the crowd, ducking down if anyone she knew looked her way. People began mingling and dancing, and Lizzie kept moving toward the barn door. She just needed to avoid Sarah and her friends most of all. And her parents. Maybe she'd just tell everyone she was sick or something. Lizzie perked up—in fact, as she was walking out the barn door she decided she could pretend she was about to throw up. Lizzie wasn't fond of lying or making stories up to get out of things—but the situation was dire. No matter what, she did not want to get on that stage. Her whole body hummed with the purpose of getting far, far away from the spotlight.

Just as she had the thought, the band stopped playing and her mom stood on the makeshift stage and took the microphone.

"Everyone, everyone!" she said, her loud voice made even louder by the microphone and the echo in the barn. "Hello! Welcome to our Valentine's Day party! All proceeds go to the running of this orchard, so we can't thank you enough for celebrating the love of our community and this beautiful place we're in."

Lizzie knew this was her chance. Her mom could talk a lot, and Lizzie could sneak out before she was done. She was so close to the barn door. She just had a few more people to get around.

"But we're also celebrating one of the finest, most beautiful of emotions," her mother continued. "One that can make you write poetry, smile like a goofball, and make you even . . . sing songs! And boy, do I have a treat for you tonight. Please welcome my daughter Lizzie to the stage to start off the romance—and who knows what else!—with one of the best love songs of all time!"

Lizzie stopped in her tracks. She felt her eyes go wide. A spotlight from somewhere found her in the crowd and suddenly she couldn't move. "Come on up here, honey!" her mom said into the microphone.

The crowd started clapping and cheering, but Lizzie's legs felt like concrete. People around her nudged her toward the stage, and though she felt as if she barely moved her legs, she found herself walking up the steps and standing next to her mother. The lights were so bright, it took her a minute to adjust. She looked down at the huge crowd all staring up at her. Someone handed her a microphone, but Lizzie hardly felt it. IT had happened: Lizzie was now standing in the middle of her worst nightmare.

CHAPTER 18
Something to Say

The whole audience had gone quiet. Lizzie saw Sarah and her friends smiling at her and Sarah mouthing, "GO ON." She could hear her own breath way too fast and loud in the microphone, and a loud squeak sounded from microphone feedback. Aaron said quietly, "Are you ready, Lizzie?" Without waiting for her reply, the band played the first notes of "Can't Help Falling in Love."

Lizzie had no words. Now she really felt like she might throw up. Her throat was dry and she couldn't open her mouth. Her face burned and tears sprang to her eyes. Her cue came up, but instead of singing, Lizzie dropped the microphone, ran down the stage steps, and sprinted out of the barn.

The cool night air hit her hard on the way out, but it felt good. She ran and ran and ran, to one of her favorite trees in the orchard. One that even her friends—even Sarah—didn't know about. She could hear people calling her name, but she dropped down under the tree and caught her breath. And as she caught her breath, the tears started flowing.

She had no idea how she would ever be able to look at anyone again. But the bigger feeling she had was anger. Anger that she'd been pushed into this. Anger that no one had listened to her. Anger that she hadn't even wanted to be a part of the schemes to begin with.

She kicked her foot on the ground in frustration. Then, almost as soon as it had started, the anger turned to hurt. She was just . . . hurt.

Her body deflated. Anger had felt better. Hurt felt really sad.

She looked back at the events of the past few weeks. She felt like her friends—even Peter—didn't listen to her concerns. They only wanted what they wanted. And Sarah had bulldozed over her like usual. But this time it didn't sit right with Lizzie. She had feelings too. And they were just as important—Mr. Samson had said so. Didn't her friends have any idea how she would feel? Or her parents? In fact, the only person who seemed to know her was her sister, of all people.

But then Gloria's words echoed in her head: "People can't read your mind."

She leaned against the rough bark of the tree and started to calm down. She took deep breaths and let the cool air wash over her. And suddenly, things became clear. She remembered another thing Mr. Samson had said—it was her choice, always, what she did with her voice.

Lizzie had come to a decision. She wiped her eyes and got up. And then walked back to the barn.

The music had started playing again, and when she walked in, no one really noticed. But she didn't stop at the door. She walked all the way up the steps to the stage and stood right in the middle. She could hear Mr. Samson's voice in the back of her mind, and that made her stand up straighter. The band died down and Lizzie took the microphone.

People murmured among themselves and a steady stream of voices filled the sudden silence from the band. Lizzie had their attention—but also didn't, really. Everyone was talking now. Suddenly, a long, loud whistle sounded through the room. She heard Gloria's voice yell, "LISTEN UP, PEOPLE. LIZZIE HAS THE MIC." She looked around until she found Gloria in the crowd and saw that she had a huge smile on her face. Gloria put both thumbs up and winked at Lizzie. Then she put on her sunglasses and pretended not to pay attention to her.

Lizzie smiled and felt her confidence grow.

Her body relaxed. Her throat opened up. And she spoke into the mic. "I have something to say!" she said, her voice shaking. But she didn't care. She did have something to say. And it was just as important as everyone else's thoughts.

"I really like singing, and I have a good voice, but I did NOT want to sing this song tonight. No one asked me what I really wanted! No one ever does. So I'm going to tell you, because no one can read my mind. And because my thoughts are important. Mom and Dad: I really didn't want singing lessons. I like Mr. Samson and I want to keep doing it, but next time, let ME decide what I get to do. Or at least take into account what I think. And Sarah—you never really listened to what I thought about your plans to get your mom and Sheriff Hadley engaged. So I'll tell you—it's not a good idea! And Peter and Olive, you knew these plans were a bad idea. We talked about it! But you still went ahead because you had your own ideas of what you wanted to happen. These aren't good reasons to do things. We should LISTEN to what people have to say. And be up-front about things. But even without listening, ANYONE can see that they're not ready to get married! Right, Sheriff Hadley and Ms. Shirvani?"

The two of them were standing in the middle of the crowd, both with shocked expressions. The barn was totally quiet. Sarah moved up beside her mom. "Well, I guess the cat's out of the bag," Sarah said, then stared hard at Lizzie. "But we were just trying to make it easy for you guys to get married. I know about you and I think it's great!"

Ms. Shirvani looked around with her mouth

open. "Well . . . I wasn't . . ." Then she seemed to get her bearings. "Okay, I wasn't expecting this to be so public," she said, turning around to look at everyone. "And I'm so glad, honey, that you approve! We can talk about this later. But right now, I'll just say Lizzie is right!"

Sarah stepped back like the words had smacked her in the face. Her eyebrows furrowed. "But . . . I thought you guys had been together for a while. Don't you want to take the next step?"

Ms. Shirvani smiled at Sarah and pushed some of her hair behind her ear. Then she turned to Sheriff Hadley. "You know I love you, Colin, but I don't want to get married. Not yet, anyway."

The sheriff, whose face was bright red, took off his hat and said, "Oh, Ana, I feel the exact same way. We've got plenty of time! I'm not going anywhere." He looked at Sarah. "We should have told you, Sarah. We can talk about this later, for sure. I think we definitely owe you an explanation. And probably lots of ice cream." Then Ms. Shirvani and the sheriff turned to each other and kissed.

Lizzie turned back to the microphone while they were kissing. She avoided looking at her friends. She had just one more thing to say. "Also, as for singing . . . well, I get to choose when I share that. And that's not tonight."

She put the microphone back in the stand, trudged down the steps, and ran out of the barn for the second time that night.

And she'd never felt better than she did at that moment.

CHAPTER 19
Talking It Through

L izzie walked into the cool night air again, but she didn't get very far before she felt a hand on her arm. Her mother turned her around and engulfed her in a huge hug.

She didn't know where they came from, but suddenly Lizzie felt tears on her cheeks once again. And then she was sobbing. She hadn't realized how upset she was until her mother hugged her.

"Oh, honey," her mom said, stroking her hair. "I'm so, so proud of you for speaking up!"

Lizzie cried harder. When she finally felt the tears subsiding, she backed up and said, "Really?"

She hadn't seen her dad come up, but suddenly he was there and he put his arm around her. "Of COURSE we are. That was why we wanted you to take singing lessons in the first place!" he said. "But it seems like we went about it the wrong way."

Lizzie smiled a little. "Well, I did really like them. I'm glad I went after all."

Her mom said, "I'm glad, honey. And we're always going to push you to try new things. But next time, we'll sit down and talk with you about it and come to an agreement. Does that sound good?"

Lizzie felt the tears come back but nodded.

She liked that idea a lot. Ms. Shirvani and Sheriff Hadley joined her parents, and Ms. Shirvani gave her a big hug.

"You're such a sensitive soul, Lizzie. We're so grateful for you. But sometimes sensitive souls have to let people know when they're being hurt. And you did that! That's hard."

Her parents nodded and so did the sheriff, and Lizzie felt like crying yet again. But then the sheriff said, "And don't worry—we will NOT ask you to sing if we decide to get married."

Lizzie giggled, and her parents laughed hard. Her mother nudged her with her shoulder and said, "It looks like there are others who want to talk to you." Lizzie looked toward the barn door, and her three friends were standing there, staring at her. Sarah looked angry; Olive looked confused; and Peter looked sympathetic.

She really didn't want to go talk to them. Especially Sarah. This all seemed so intense, and part of her still felt really worried about telling people how she felt. It needed to be done. But it was super-uncomfortable for her. Still, she made her legs start walking and moved toward her friends.

Before she even got there, Sarah said, "I can't believe . . . How could . . ." Lizzie stopped in front of her and watched as Sarah tried to find words—normally never a problem.

"Sarah, I'm sorry I didn't say something earlier. I should have," Lizzie said. "But I feel like you steamroller over me and don't listen when I do say things. It seems like you only want to hear what you want to hear. And then you just move forward without really asking me what I think."

Sarah huffed out a breath and crossed her arms. But she didn't say anything and just continued to glare.

Peter stepped up. "You were right about thinking of other people when we were doing things. I got caught up in the idea that *I* could be the one to make people happy. But that's not the point. I should have listened to you, Lizzie. I still feel bad about how some of our operations turned out."

Olive pushed her glasses up. "Yeah, people aren't experiments. I should know that by now. I should have listened too."

Lizzie said, "I'm just as much to blame. I didn't try that hard to say what I wanted to say. And anyway, we were all just trying to do something nice for Sarah."

Just as she finished her sentence, David, one of Peter and Olive's dads, came up to the group. "What a night!" he said. "Lizzie, I don't think I've ever heard you say that much at one time."

Peter and Olive giggled, and Lizzie did too, a little bit. But her face got hot and she looked down.

"I'm going to take these two troublemakers home. John has a whole Valentine's Day dictionary game planned out." David winked at Lizzie. "It's nice to hear you speak out, Lizzie."

She smiled. Peter and Olive gave her a hug and then they hugged Sarah, who still looked like a volcano about to blow. Peter, Olive, and

David walked away, leaving Lizzie alone with Sarah. Who was practically vibrating. Lizzie turned to her.

Sarah said in a low voice, "So this is all my fault?"

Lizzie shook her head. "No, I'm not saying that—"

Sarah went on. "You just did! You were all doing something nice for me, remember? And you were SO NICE to me tonight that you told my secret to an entire barn full of people. And now my mom and the sheriff aren't getting engaged. What a good friend you are!"

Lizzie could hardly believe her ears. She took a deep breath. "Look, I am really sorry for the way I handled this. I should have said something a lot earlier. But, Sarah, your mom and the sheriff aren't ready! Did you not hear them?"

Sarah went on, "If you'd just sung the song like you were supposed to, none of this would have happened. If you'd just been a good friend—"

Lizzie felt her voice come up from her diaphragm. "YOU AREN'T LISTENING, SARAH. You just do whatever you want all the time and you don't LISTEN TO ME. For once in your life, really hear what I have to say. The sheriff is going to be in your life. Now that this is out in the open, things will be different and you will basically have what you want. Only, no one gets hurt this way! How can you not see that this is a good thing? I know I shouldn't have announced it at the barn. I know I should have said something sooner. But now I'm talking and you have to listen! And then hear this: I AM a good friend. I am a REALLY good friend. In fact, I'm your BEST friend. So I think you should start treating me like it!"

And for the third time in one night, Lizzie walked away. But this time with her shoulders back and her head held high.

CHAPTER 20
Belting It Out

Lizzie tossed in her bed again. She hadn't heard from Sarah all night. And hadn't heard from her the following morning. So she lay in bed thinking about how saying things to people could be really painful. And had the potential of losing best friends.

There was a knock on her door and she yelled, "Come in!" Her heart raced—she really hoped it would be Sarah.

Instead, Gloria opened the door and came in. Without asking, she sat down on the chair in the corner.

"Wow, when you decide to tell people off, you really tell people off," she said. Lizzie groaned and put her knees up to her chest. She put her head on her knees. Then she looked up.

"Is everyone talking about it?" she asked.

Gloria examined a fingernail. "Let's just say that more than a few people have texted asking for the details of your . . . meltdown."

Lizzie's head snapped up. "It wasn't a meltdown!" she said. "Those things were important to say." Though, lying in her bed and looking at the ceiling, she had wondered if it was worth it. What good was it to tell people your feelings if you lost your best friend?

Gloria suddenly grinned. "It was spectacular."

Lizzie heard the sound of speaker and micro-phone feedback outside her window. She looked at Gloria, who said, "I came in to tell you that your fan club is outside. You might want to go see what they want." She got up and walked out the door.

Then she stuck her head back in. "And Lizzie. I'm really proud of you. That was pretty cool last night." She looked Lizzie up and down. "Put on some real clothes before you go out. Don't embarrass me."

As Gloria disappeared, the sounds outside turned into . . . a song. One of Lizzie's favorite songs.

The opening music started to "You've Got a Friend in Me." But then something even better happened: she heard Sarah singing the opening lines.

Lizzie ran to the window and looked out. Sarah had a portable karaoke machine and stood right outside her window. Peter and Olive stood behind Sarah, giggling and doing a funny dance to the song. Sarah belted out, "You've got a friend in me!" And pointed at Lizzie.

Lizzie felt tears come to her eyes. But these were happy tears. She threw on some clothes and ran out the door.

When she came out, Sarah gave her a look—a look that said "I'm sorry." She finished a line of the song and then put the microphone under Lizzie's mouth for her to sing. Without hesitating, Lizzie sang, loudly, "YOU'VE GOT A FRIEND IN ME!"

She would absolutely share her voice with her friends. From now on.

The song ended and Sarah turned off the karaoke machine.

"Lizzie," Sarah said, her eyes brimming. "I'm sorry. I thought about what you said yesterday. I really, really heard what you said. I talked to my mom and the sheriff and things are really good now. I should have done that from the beginning—I should have LISTENED to you from the beginning. But I want you to know that I always want to hear what you say. I promise! And I asked Peter and Olive to tell me when I'm getting too steamroller-y."

Olive pushed up her glasses and grinned. "One of my favorite things to do," she said.

Peter said, "But we ALL will tell each other

the things we need to hear. And we'll always listen to each other."

Sarah moved forward to Lizzie. "I'm sorry I called you a bad friend. You're an amazing friend. I only said that because I was mad."

Lizzie smiled. "I know. And we both had things to apologize for. But best friends forgive each other and learn and keep going!" She put her arms out and Sarah gave her a huge hug, and then Olive and Peter joined them. They all toppled over on the ground.

Then, like they had all planned it, they all started singing "You've Got a Friend in Me" at the top of their lungs, laughing the whole way through.

Peter and Olive started their funny dance

again and Sarah and Lizzie joined in. Lizzie couldn't stop laughing—she hadn't felt this free in weeks. She belted out the song as loudly as she could.

Gloria strode out of the house, her sunglasses on and her boa flung around her neck. Sarah, Peter, Olive, and Lizzie saw her all at the same time and stopped singing. She looked really mad.

Gloria walked over to them, her mouth in a straight line, and Lizzie braced for whatever mean thing she was going to say. She guessed this was one of Gloria's mood swings, and she sighed in resignation.

Gloria marched up to Lizzie and took off her sunglasses. "You, BABY"—she started in a stern voice, then smiled—"have a pretty good voice. But I think you need this." She wrapped the boa around Lizzie, who stood stunned.

"There," Gloria said. "Now you can look as good as you sound." Then she walked back into the house, leaving all four of them shocked.

Lizzie regained her composure and turned to her three friends. She flipped the boa around her shoulders. "What do you think? Should we go sing some more?"

Sarah, Peter, and Olive all said at the same time, "You've got a friend in me, Lizzie!"

Lizzie knew she did. And she knew that from now on, she could use her voice to say whatever she needed to say. She couldn't wait to tell Mr. Samson.

She walked into the house with Sarah, Olive, and Peter, tapped on the banister three times, and went into the living room to sing her heart out with her three best friends in the whole wide world.

ACKNOWLEDGMENTS

This series has been so fun to write, and I couldn't have done it without my awesome editor, Emma Sector. I will miss you, Emma! Thank you for your keen eyes, your kind words, and your unerring ability to steer these projects in the right direction.

I couldn't have even started this without my amazing agent, Ammi-Joan Paquette, who has been a fantastic champion and cheerleader. And without the support of my friends and family, I would have never been able to finish these. Thank you to all of the awesome people in my life!

ABOUT THE AUTHOR

MEGAN ATWOOD is an author and an assistant professor at Rowan University whose most recent books include the Dear Molly, Dear Olive series. When she's not writing books for kids of all ages, she's making new friends, going on zombie hayrides, and visiting haunted houses. And, always, petting her two adorable cats, who "help" her write every book.